Large Format Paper Edition
Continuous Printing
First Published January 24, 2014
Reissue E, January 14, 2025

Library of Congress
Control Number: 2016902891

ISBN: 9780983857594

Published by
WEST WINTER PRESS
Sky Valley, California, USA

love in bed

love stories by

j.j.kirnan

From the Author

I have long known I would write a book of sexual episodes, each with a different couple, in the mode of literary fiction. I intended them to be love stories.

This book is my offering, twenty-one moments, each a slow ballet between romantic lovers or a torrid frenzy of sex. Often, both.

With love and sex in the same bed, neither shy, "It's too much," some say. "I can't take it."

Also heard: "Less is more."

I chose more.

I suggest encountering each as a separate song or poem – a lyric interlude in a pillow-book rather than an on-rushing chapter of an impetuous novel.

Read one. Close the book. Open again when you can't keep your hands off.

John Kirnan
North Atlantic Shoreline
Spring, 2016

Formatting note

Normally, an edition of fiction is formatted with equal length lines. This requires hyphenation, yet even that cannot fully remedy odd spacing.

For *Love In Bed*, I have chosen to leave the ends of sentences ragged, which allows each word and letter proper spacing, enables the font to display authentically.

This is suitable, I believe, for prose that often flirts with the freedoms of poetry.

jjk

contents

delightful

sorrowful

ecstatic

delightful

his wild will
oh carolina
a pear
all the way happy again
roared off the downslope
the simple shift of things
too bright to believe in

his wild will

"**D**id you check the temp?"
"1-0-3."
"Perfect. It'll get to 1-0-9 this afternoon, hotter tomorrow."

They continued packing for Palm Springs. Friends in Los Angeles were horrified they liked to visit the desert in summer. 'Hideous,' was the particular opinion of his sister. Never mind, they both prized the brutal dry furnace of the Sonoran Desert.

Then he noticed her sneaking something into the large suitcase, something strictly *verboten*.

"Whoa whoa whoa. What's that?"

"What?"

"Come on!"

"All right, all right." She dragged a black dress out onto the bed.

"Okay, let's go over this again," he said, scolding like a disgusted schoolteacher.

"I know, I'm bad, aren't I," she replied with charming pretend guilt.

"Why are we going?"

"Sleeping in. Baking, hot as we can stand it, swimming, hot tub, and sex."

"That's right. And that's all. We have to come back in 48 hours, for God's sake."

"What if there's an emergency?"

"An emergency where you need a fancy black dress?"

"It could be a gastronomical crisis."

"I swear I'm going duct tape the door the second we get in."

She smiled prettily. "By tomorrow night it won't matter how much of all that you've done, you're going to want to go out for dinner, I know you will. I can't go in my bikini."

"We'll have them deliver."

"Just out to Pesca. No shopping. No movies."

"Oh, man ..."

"Those shrimp, you've got to have them right out of the kitchen."

"You're going off the plan, you're going off the plan," he wailed insincerely.

"And then we'll go straight back to the room, so you can fuck me."

He stopped dead. She wore an innocent smile, but with mischief in the corners of it.

"What?"

She looked right in his eyes, she who never used this word, and said it slowly. "Take me back to the hotel and fuck me." No blink.

The shock of it zapped full strength up the

optic and aural nerves, to explode in the hypothalamus, the primitive brain, which jolted him erect in two seconds.

"I cannot believe you said that. You never say that."

"What?" She eased away from her side of the bed. Around it. Toward him.

"What you said."

She took two more steps. "You mean, 'fuck me'?"

He nodded.

"Fuck me." One shoulder shrugged, and the strap of her top slipped down her arm. She moved gracefully to stand three feet away. She held his eyes with total intention.

"Fuck me."

Disbelief vanished. Mr. Hypothalamus seized control. They crashed together. Her arms around his neck pulled him in. Her hungry mouth invaded his. Her shorts fit loosely at the thigh and his hand went right up one leg to grasp soft flesh and pull it against his body. She understood this. She un-kissed ...

"Use both hands."

Now he controlled her lower body, squeezing her bottom, rocking her pelvis against his erection. She grasped the hem of her tank top and yanked it up and off, quickly dispensing of her bra, which unfastened at the front. He kept trying to interfere the whole time with his mouth on her shoulders. She wrapped her arms around

his neck, pressed her breasts against him, and
opened her mouth under his, pulling his head
with one hand, urging the kiss as deep as possible.
Truly crazy deep.

She yanked away, completely out of his arms.

"Don't move," she said.

In two jolting seconds, she bent over, dragged
her shorts and underwear together down over
hips and off. Naked. She pushed the suitcase off
the bed.

"Don't move," she whispered. "I'm going to
say it again, I can feel it coming. When I say it,
take off your clothes and do it."

He nodded, staggered by her bold ways and
red-hot heat as he might have conjured it in an
angelic dream.

She moved to the bed, turning her back to
him, and began to climb on, stopping, resting on
all fours. Slowly, gracefully, she eased backwards
toward him, to the edge, as far as possible
without falling off. Her torso lowered onto the
bed, bottom remaining high. One knee moved to
the right almost three feet. Her left hand slipped
between thighs and began to caress the labial
folds, slowly, with deliberate sensuality. He
could see everything, so open did she make it. He
could barely breathe.

"Now," she whispered, "fuck me."

It took four seconds to shed his clothing. He
stared at her open sex the whole time. She
continued caressing, making the lips separate,

revealing the light pinkish flesh deeper in.

"Fuck me here," she whispered.

He moved to the edge of the bed, placed the tip of his cock between the lips and sank home.

"Ohhmmoh," she cried out plaintively, the soaring-song of penetration. How good it sounded.

His strokes, at first deliberate, accelerated with the roar of his wild will. Her surrendered position made him ache – legs spread, back curved to put bottom high in the air – the unashamed offering of sex that makes a man greedy.

He reveled in everything held apart for him. How mighty to wedge her open, the heft of his cock splitting her wide. Wet – her insides the viscosity of slushing cream, melting. He plunged in with power in rhythm, each stroke greeted with a grunt, a squeal, or the wicked-sweet f-profanity never heard from her lips before.

Then – only that blind overwhelm, that bursting open, that shooting. His primitive brain screamed for joy, nerve ends sparking off, the fireworks of infinity in blastoff release, for seconds, seconds, bursting in body and face from emptying.

He collapsed forward, pushing her flat onto the bed. The saturation of his brain with the chemistry of pleasure lifted him high, floating, so good.

Drifting down, he was aware of her laughing

gently. She had squirmed out from beneath, flipped onto her side, and pulled her knees to her chest, looking in his eyes. She seemed full of delight. Heaving, gradually recovering his breath, he waited for her to say something. She knelt up on the bed with her thighs closed, hands resting on them.

"Where am I?" he got out, finally.

She just smiled down at him, like the Sphinx pleased with the spring flood of the Nile.

"That was amazing," he said.

She looked down for a second or two more. Abruptly, she jumped off the bed.

"Quick," she whispered.

He sat up. She was already pulling her shorts back on.

"Don't you want to melt into the bed for a while?" he said. "I'm spent."

"Quick," she said again, making a sign to him to get dressed.

"Can't."

"I'll drive," she said.

"Was that good ... did you ..."

She sat on the edge of the bed looking right at him, bare breasts ludicrously causing another stir in his bottomless libido. "I'm glad I didn't. All the hotter. Let's go to the desert. I hope it goes to one-eleven tomorrow."

He stared in disbelief. She leaned over a little closer. "I'm glad I didn't. I can feel it buzzing and throbbing. Hope it stays like that all the way to

Palm Springs. I might even touch myself while I drive." She yanked her tank-top on.

He just shook his head and tried to get dressed. Whatever the Nile had served up for breakfast, he hoped it delivered ample leftovers. She finished packing both suitcases and set them next to the door.

"I wasn't watching. Did you put the dress in?"

She gave him the biggest smile. "Uh-huh."

"We'll go get shrimps?"

"Uh-huh."

She stopped smiling and looked right in his eyes.

"Then take me back to the hotel and fuck me."

oh carolina

It stopped raining.

She sighed. "What's really annoying about it, suddenly too many choices. First none, then one, now too many."

"That's good annoy, right?" he asked.

She looked over at him with no smile. "Okay, buddy, I need to rant. Full speed ahead. Ya gonna catch me out on every little thing like that?"

"I could, but that would be annoying."

She sent an unconvincing scowl.

"All right, all right," he said, "I'm backing off. I'm your listener."

Her spill and ramble resumed on the porch of their Blue Ridge Mountain cabin.

Early spring was a muddy affair here, twenty miles north and a bit east of Asheville, but they treasured it anyway. They were not attempting any work in the woods this weekend – it was an inside job. She had asked him to stand with support while she made a big career decision. He liked the assignment – the one you love with mind in motion. Irresistible.

She was so voluble. He listened while she ticked off the pros and cons of an exciting job offer, Research Director at the main library in Charlotte. This was a Big Deal. Powerful Credential. The position had been highly contested, and the news yesterday of a for-real contract offer lit her up. He injected a point here and there. Just points, not advice.

"I timed the drive," she said.

"Yeah?"

"Nine minutes."

"So, this library thing is your front runner?"

She resumed ranging the pros and cons of the offer, sinking deeper into each factor. He followed the whole thing, amazingly. Then she turned her guns on a different opportunity, new eight days ago. Behind that were two less specific options – but nonetheless plausible – for launching her on a fast track to a doctorate, faster than the library job would, certainly. These last two had come to ground because of an unexpected resignation in an adjacent department of her school's library, a 'would you be interested were an offer to appear' conversation with an academic colleague, and a talk with her long-time mentor three days ago.

Many choices.

"Make me lunch," she said after a quiet

moment.

"Omelet, tuna sandwich, some of that soup from last night, or me?"

"I think of you as dessert."

"I could be higher up the menu than that," he said.

She came across the edge of the deck toward him, holding his gaze, putting arms around him. "Did you notice something?"

"What?"

"None of these gets in our way."

"I did notice that." They were all in Charlotte, and none far across town.

They formed the first important kiss of the day. It was bigger than life.

"Only nine minutes, huh?"

"Yup."

"More time in the morning."

"Yup."

"We like the morning."

"Yup."

His wisdom knew she would speak up if decision-making needed to remain undisturbed by acts of physical love. Therefore, sex is on the table, as per always. Therefore, his kiss, just then, remained undiluted. She moved beautifully in it, angling her head, responding to his pressures, tangling tongues with him. It was warm as spring.

Soon they were standing face to face on the deck with some clothing discarded. She pressed

against his bare chest, even if hers was not
naked, knowing he liked that half-undressed
tease for a while before worshiping her fully,
there. He kissed her mouth with persistence.
Her hair flowed around her shoulders. He
positioned his hand under it on her neck, not
to control, just to feel the will, the intention in
her, the assertion in her, as she moved in the
kissing.

"All this talking makes me oral," she
whispered between times. "And kissing. Kisses
make my oral ... oral."

They moved inside to escape the chill in the
North Carolina April air. She took his hand
and walked over to the bed. At its edge they
kissed long, again. He loved their turns,
holding his mouth centered on hers while she
kissed up and under his lips, then deeper, with
quick little nibbles and ever more salacious
incursions deeper. She was inventive with that
lush mouth of hers, his smart, adorable mate.
Each time the buildup of tension from her turn
overwhelmed, he took his turn.

*I hope this contest lasts to the end, with the
outcome in doubt.*

Finally, laughing, she pushed him down on
the bed.

"What is this, a necking party?" she asked,
sarcasm thick.

"You require foreplay."

"You do."

"You." He stripped off his jeans and every other stitch while she stood with hands on hips watching. Without a hint of embarrassment, she deliberately bent the focus of her being on his jutting cock when it came free. When it moved, her head moved, tracking.

"Lay down. Lay still," she ordered.

"Aren't you taking your clothes off?"

She didn't answer. The cock had her full attention. She edged forward. He felt the disturbing sensation of being stalked by a tenacious hungry thing in the wild. Suddenly it leapt on his naked body, pinned him down with its legs, and administered the attack sure to bring victory – his cock engulfed by its hungry mouth.

"Oh, Carolina!"

She was very good. Oh, this girl was most excellent indeed. Just award the doctorate now, honorarily, honestly, hopelessly, happily. Her mouth engulfing him, sucking on him, sliding him in, that mouth making love to him.

"Like that, right there, right there."

She drew off, laughing with bright eyes looking up in his.

"Where?"

"Don't stop!"

"I love it in my mouth."

"Oh man ..."

"I love it all the way in."

"Don't stop."

"I can go deeper."

"Oh my God."

She put it back in. She slid her tongue around and teased the head with the underside of lips. Every few moments she let it sink deep, all the way to the back of her throat. Sometimes it went deep down in, and he moaned like a wounded beast.

Abruptly, she abandoned the attack and jumped off the bed.

"My other mouth is going to make you very happy now." Arching her torso and with head tilted away to get hair behind, her hands went to the front of her undergarment and unfastened it, revealing to him his other favorite part of her. Parts of her.

She pulled off the rest of her clothes while he watched.

"Beautiful fucking naked girl in the woods."

"That's right."

She swung on top. She looked down at her hands guiding his erection. The head of it gently eased the lips apart. She let her weight fall, to effect the penetration. It made a lusty sound.

"I consent," he said. She gave a blustering laugh.

He recognized the signs – she wished to stay on top. Her movements signaled positioning to maximize her pleasure. The right rub. That was still unselfish – it only required a tiny percent of her shimmy to raise him.

Sometimes she made him slide out, then positioned the labial lips – just so – against the shaft, and rocked like mad, to inflame the lips and the wonderful glans at the top of them. Then, looking in his eyes, she nestled the head back in the opening and slithered all the way down on it, all the way impaled, and used the strong muscle inside to squeeze.

"Oh man oh man oh man oh man oh man."

"I love rubbing us together." She took him out again, slid herself all over his cock, wet, slippery, and so warm.

"Take me to the end," he said.

Then – drama. She froze, with one hand on his organ. Her eyes gripped his. He held his breath.

"Chase me down in the stacks next week."

"What!?"

"I know what corner to run to. Chase me. Push me up against the books and enter me from behind. I want to be taken in the library."

She lowered her sex onto his, letting her weight tell, letting her organs melt around him. Her orgasm was not far away. She uttered his name with liquid heat.

"No underwear under your skirts," he managed to say, as they let loose the endgame.

"I made love with the sexy librarian."

"Not yet. I'm still undecided."

"Married the Librarian."

"Oh my god I'm serious never never never never or I'll kill you don't ever call me 'Marion the Librarian' never never ever."

"What? She's cute."

"Never never never." She looked fierce.

He paused for a moment, to gain advantage.

"Okay, I promise."

"Thank God."

"Can I ask why not?"

"Marion would never get to be on top like that."

a pear

Once more, gratitude surfaced for the separation a rural location provides – their house sat out on the edge of things, no other within four hundred yards. Hedges and trees across the front of the property formed a natural barrier. Privacy.

They stood on the front porch, close but not touching. The sun descended over the Ohio summer day.

"... still warm for a while," she said quietly. "You're not ready to go inside, are you?"

"No."

They had been talking and kissing since she woke from a nap. Also – removing each other's garments. It was serious.

"I like getting you out of your clothes," he said, summing up the situation.

She nodded "Yes. Seems. Somehow, I'm naked again. It keeps happening."

"I don't need to try very hard."

She agreed with a slow shake of her head, hair shifting across shoulders.

"You stand right there."

"Okay," he said.

She moved away. The long hair, brown as the dark half of a chestnut, slid across her back. He appreciated her body – the tapered waist below the cascade of hair, the curve of hip, the roundness of bottom. She was a pear, full on hips and thighs, long-waisted but not tall, small on top. Legs proportional, strong, not thick.

Her body-style kindled his libido. He loved it unconditionally.

She glided across the porch, turned slightly, and stood still. In slow motion, she lowered into a crouch. One hand reached for a skirt crumpled on the deck and sought something in a pocket. She rose and stopped.

"Stay there," she reminded without a glance.

A turn, as if a stately dance – she faced around and closed the distance between them to eight feet, halted, stood solid. She would not look at him.

She arched her torso, laid her head back and shook it, causing the abundance of hair to sway and form up. Her hands rose to her head, slipped along her face and behind, gathering stray tresses, gaining a grasp on the fine mane. She put it up. Red bands taken from the skirt pocket kept handfuls in place. Some ends stuck out. A quick flick of the wrist twisted a braid-like strand behind, which she tucked into place. Inevitably, a few rebellious wisps escaped capture, long, silky, floating in the early evening air.

All the while, the elevation of arms and tilt of body unashamedly presented her breasts, a sweet-hot tease that inflamed madly.

She lowered her arms and stood half turned away, looking off the porch into the yard. She whispered without looking over.

"Stay there."

An impish smile played on her lips. He believed she avoided looking at him because the sight of the male organ – fat, hard, pointing practically straight up – would have ended her aloof theatrical.

She drifted to her right and bent at the waist to reach down. She could put her hands completely flat on the floor without bending her knees, an astonishing thing.

She took his blue shirt in hand and rose. Two steps further to the left. A repeat of the full bending from the waist to retrieve a pair of yellow cotton pants. Up again, a swivel, and down, including a sideways bend and arch in her neck to make his view of her rounding and falling breasts unimpeded.

This sexy-girl ballet – including two more repeats to get a sock and jeans – had transpired in slow motion, a maddening, provoking display that tugged at his appetites.

Another sock lay two steps down the stairs leading to the front lawn. She bent over from the deck with knees straight, and like an animal going beyond limits, extended ten inches below her feet to retrieve it with tips of fingers.

Breathtaking.

Moving across the floor again, she let the sock fall. An extra bending and getting was necessary to remedy the disaster. Finally, she padded to the swing ten feet from him, leaned over and made a neat pile of their clothing.

Apparently having achieved domestic tranquility, an expression of consternation to the contrary came over her face. "Oh dear," she said with mock horror that almost made him laugh out loud. She was looking down at one piece neglected in the roundup – her white top lying four feet in front of him. She started toward it, gliding, passed to the side of it, and started a turn. She stopped short. She locked on his erection.

"Oh dear."

This time he did laugh.

"Hold a minute, I have to get this," she said, one arm pointing down to the floor. But instead of bending to get the shirt, her gaze ripped away from his sex and flit up his body to meet his eyes.

"I love it when you look at me," she said.

"Yes?"

"I like to be naked and show everything."

"I could watch a long time," he managed to say. His hand surrounded his organ.

"Do you like it when I bend over?

"Yes."

"I like to do it front ways and back ways," she said.

"Yes."

"Can you see anything in between when I bend over?"

"Yes, if your legs are a little apart, I can see the lips pressed together, a little hill with a line between."

"Does that look good?

"Yes. And your bottom is intensely cute. Seeing it naked makes me hard." He stroked his organ.

She blushed. Her eyes grew fiery. She let him see how it got through her defenses and made her feel sexy, the comments about her body.

"I can feel your eyes going on my breasts all the time."

"Like now?" He looked at them deliberately. She arched a little to urge them up and forward. They were exactly right and ripe for a pear.

"Yes," she said. "I like you looking at them. You said ... how many times did you say they're not too small?"

"Forty thousand times," he said.

They were silent for a while as he admired her. Her femme pride waited for him to speak. He did.

"They are perfect."

She fit one hand at the base of the right one, lifted it slightly, saying nothing.

"Are you going to put your hands on the floor again?"

She smiled. "You like that?"

"A lot," he said.

"Well, I have to pick up my shirt, can't just leave it lying around, you know."

"Right."

She rotated until her back squared up to him. She shifted her wide hips side to side, then angled her head around to look at him one last time. Turning back, she bent at the waist, slowly. Her bottom rounded. Her hands reached the floor. She moved one leg a step to the left and let her palms lie flat on the wood deck of the porch, fingers splaying. She swayed her hips again, halves of her bottom sliding up and down, with everything in between offered, open.

"I love you looking."

One hand remained on the floor. The other rose to the mouth of her sex. She slipped fingers around it, opening it as if exposing a flower.

"I love you looking at me," she said. "I'm wet from you looking. Put it in."

He moved behind. He had to position his feet outside her hips and bend his knees, adjusting to find the angle. He rubbed the head of his erection all over the outer lips, making her fingers wet where she held the lips spread.

"Put it in," she said again, with sweet-pathos-begging in it.

And there in the evening of the Midwest in summer, on the porch of their home, they coupled very well indeed. She made her stance steady. The strength of her sturdy body in that position thrilled, both hands on the floor to drive back into each thrust. She absorbed his strength and power and his inexorable drive to penetrate – lust she had incited with bold behavior.

She voiced the battle, one cry each stroke, looking over her shoulder.

"In. Yes. Yes. Yes. Fuck. Me. Break. Me. Hard. Fuck. Me. Hard. Fuck. Fuck. Fuck."

Her words grabbed at her breath. Each pounding seemed intent on driving her into the ground, his relentless attack making her body heave forward and her breasts shudder. He was strong, and proved it for a full minute at full speed.

"Harder. Fuck me. Harder."

Instead, he paused, thrusting once deep to keep her pinned, chest heaving to gather fire for more. She smiled into his eyes over her shoulder, holding position. She whispered with the wiles of the good witch ...

"Get me naked like this. Naked. Make me show off, make me bend over. Make me open my body on the floor under you. Take me from behind." She paused for drama, waiting. Waiting ... whispering even quieter ... "And fuck me like a warrior."

His final energies rose, a potent ball of tension welling at the base of his cock, urged into existence by her salacious talk, her creamy sex, her surrendered position. He stirred. Four, five, eight solid thrusts, each producing a grunt torn from her throat. Then the litany resumed.

"Get me wet. Fuck me." And then on each thrust ... "Fuck me, fuck me, fuck me."

Soon he knew he could finish at will, instead letting it hover, poised on the edge of eruption, just so he could slam into her another thirty times. She fell beyond words now, taking each penetration with helpless joy, grunting, squealing.

With grim satisfaction he felt her shift to climactic thrashing, still holding position, hands flat on the floor, knees straight, moans and cries desperate. She went right over the top.

"Oh my God in heaven," she screamed. Her legs failed – she sunk to her knees, shaking. He followed her down, keeping his advantage, buried deep. The warrior gave no quarter – he thrust into her helpless shivering body again and again, until the proof of victory erupted, and he bellowed into the sky.

The beautiful violence ceased. She stood in a dream, holding the bundle of their clothing pressed to her torso, inhaling the scent clinging to the fabric combined with that of her body and his on her skin. The cool evening approached, but she did not stir to escape it.

He fit behind her. For a full minute, he brushed kisses along her shoulders, at the nape of her neck, and between her shoulder blades. She absorbed them with hardly a sigh – that could be heard.

Then, she rotated to face him. Their eyes met. She lifted her right foot and set it on the edge of the porch swing. She felt him lower slightly, fit perfectly, ease her sex open, and with incredible tenderness slide his member in. She seized around it, tight, an embrace.

A beat of time with no measure.

Neither sought to inflame the other.

He withdrew with even more tenderness than the entry.

She let a tiny smile appear at the corner of her mouth, and with a glimmer in her eyes, spun away in the Ohio late afternoon, running fast into the house, their clothing still clutched to her breasts.

all the way happy again

"You could try showing up at his office with a coat on but nothing underneath," said JoAnn.

"Too risky. That's just inviting rejection and humiliation."

"How about something really wild from a smut shop online?"

"I feel really stupid in those things. I mean, how garish can you get?"

Georgia and her sister JoAnn were silent for a while, thinking.

"It's not like we never do it," Georgia said, "but it's not enough now. Not often enough."

JoAnn leaned over the table. "Georgia," she said with determination.

"What?"

"Georgia, listen to me," she said, waiting for the other's full attention. She did not continue until she obtained it, saw focus in those green eyes. "Is there another woman?"

"No," came the reply with a little heat in it.

"You wouldn't be the first woman in the world, the first attractive, desirable woman, to get dropped for some conniving little bitch, you know."

Georgia smiled in spite of her worry. "He's never away from me long enough to be having some stupid affair. Besides, I'm vigilant. We're not just strangers with an arrangement, you know. He tells me everything."

"He wouldn't tell you if his sex energy is being drained off somewhere else."

"Well, he admits that he's letting this big project get to him. Stress. That's it, it's just stress."

"They all have some big project, for God's sake. They're all under stress. He can't leave his hot beautiful wife unhappy in bed and go off to work, I'll kill him."

Georgia smiled at her sister's fierce loyalty.

"You know, JoAnn, it's partially because I need more sex, you know, just to be walking around with that glow, that jazzy feeling. But it's because I'm worried this is the start of something going downhill, something I'd look back on and say, 'You know, it all began back around the time he got that promotion and ...' well you know what I mean?"

"Yes. You should do something."

They sat there in it. Georgia sipped her iced

tea. She noticed JoAnn watching her closely with arms folded around herself.

"What?"

JoAnn didn't move.

"What?"

"I'm thinking of something a friend of mine tried. She got it from a therapist, a three-hundred-and-fifty-dollar therapist. It's pretty intense."

"Tell me, tell me."

"Georgia, this is potent stuff."

"I'm hopping up and down here in sexual frustration. Don't you think this is an emergency?"

JoAnn looked at her for another silent moment.

"The thing about this, if you really do it, it's so strong that if there is something else going on, it uncovers it, fast. Yeah, if it's something explainable, you'll get him hot, all right. But if it's something else, another woman or some hang-up or personal problem ..."

"I see."

"You've got to be ready to cope if something comes to the surface."

"Did you ever try this with Paul?"

"Modified version of."

"And?"

"Hot stuff."

"Spill. Now."

JoAnn glanced around to make sure there was

enough privacy around their table. She edged a little closer.

"Here's the logic. Sex is a good thing."

"Yes."

"It's natural and healthy and you need it to stay happy."

"Yes."

"Something is causing hubby to have low drive for the moment."

"Yes."

"You've patiently given him the chance to give a reason."

"Yes."

"If there is some emotional thing, you are his wife and he owes it to you to share it, no holding back from the wife."

"Right."

"No secrets."

"Right."

"There's no physical problem."

"No."

"There's no other woman."

"No."

"So, everything else being eliminated, and nothing you have to 'take into account,' there ought to be great sex going on."

"Yup."

"Then, what you do is, you have an affair."

"Huh?"

"You make him jealous by having an affair, a really hot sex life, right in front of him, with yourself."

"Shit."

"Here's the way my friend said the doctor put it to her: 'You have a party, it's out in the open at your house, he's invited, but no pressure, it's not mandatory, you have the most spectacular time whether he shows up or not."

"Holy cow."

"Here's the key: confidence and detachment. You're confident that there is nothing to offend him by having the party, since he says there is no problem, and since sex is normal and healthy, and since it is moral to be in 'the pursuit of your own happiness,' if you know what I mean."

"I get the picture, JoAnn."

"You're detached. You are not trying to control him into joining in. You are not trying to shame him. You are not open to guilt or shame or any kind of aggressive behaviors. You are just having a party. A wild party. Where he can see it and hear it and even smell it."

"JoAnn!"

"I told you, this is way advanced. No partying in the closet. My friend said she woke up in the middle of the night once and just started touching herself, right in the middle of the night in their bed with him one foot away."

"What happened?"

"Use your imagination."

Georgia sat there stunned, thinking about it. JoAnn leaned a little closer, as if to deliver the coup de grâce. "If there's no reason for him to stop, and you stop because he stops, how is the sex ever going to get going again?"

Georgia rocked back in her chair. She didn't say anything to JoAnn, but it occurred to her that regardless of how her husband reacted, she herself would have to process a lot of her own 'withholds' just to do it. But the logic was inescapable. She looked over at her remarkable sister.

"The man is either going to join the party in 2.3 seconds with his hot wife, or his true reason for not wanting sex is going to come out."

"You got it."

"Wow."

Suddenly JoAnn started laughing. Her hand covered her mouth.

"What now?"

"You're blushing. My sister is blushing," hooted JoAnn.

Georgia began laughing with her.

"JoAnn," she said through her smile, "I'm paying for this lunch."

The poor guy stumbled through the front door at 7:30. She gave him a sympathetic hug and a small kiss. She listened to his rant. She took his clothes off and rubbed his back well. She told a smart joke. She fed him marinated London broil and asparagus. She poured red wine. She never once wondered if he was in the mood. She laughed a lot.

He never knew what hit him.

"This is the best red we've had in months."

"Isn't it?" she agreed. "I bought three bottles. Want me to pick up a few more to have on hand?"

"Yes, definitely." He took another sip, admiring the color first. He sat draped sideways on one of the dining room chairs. "I haven't felt this relaxed in quite a while."

"Me too. This wine goes straight to my happy head," she remarked, smiling generously at him, sincerely smiling.

"Whoa."

"Straight to my lips. They're a little numb."

"You usually don't get that buzzy unless it's gin."

"Wine plus no cares makes a girl buzzy, wuzzy and wize."

"You're tipsy."

"The tipsies of my titiptsies are a little numb, too."

He sat up straight. "Georgia!"

"Wanna see 'em?"

"Georgia, are you drunk?"

She still smiled, but the look she gave him was steady and seriously risky. "My head was happy first, then the wine. I'm not drunk."

"What's going on?"

"Happy."

"Did something happen?"

She looked at him steadily. With deliberate drama, she reached over to a sideboard and fetched a pen and a sheet of paper from its top drawer, looked up at him once, and wrote a short note. She looked up again as she folded it twice over. She pushed it to the middle of the table.

"The answer to your question is in this little letter. But I'm not ready to give it to you yet." She took the empty wine bottle and set it on top of the paper. "You can read it in the morning."

"I've never seen you like this."

"I know. Now here's my plan for the evening." *Confidence and detachment, confidence and detachment.* She took a deep breath, looking right in his eyes. "I mean this with all sincerity Teddy. This has nothing to do with you. Nothing. It's just what I want to do. I'm having a party. You're invited, but you don't have to come. I mean it, I won't have even one ounce of resentment if you don't. But I need this party desperately."

"Party?"

"I'm going into the bathroom for a really great bath. Also," she slowed a little, "I'm going to find out what parts are numb and I'm going to find out what parts aren't numb at all. Not at all."

He looked stunned. She did not hook into his look. Detachment. She got up and left the table. Behind the closed door of the bathroom, she almost screamed with giddiness and thrills. It took her quite a few minutes to calm down, in fact. And to get back to home base? Where it really was just about her? That took five minutes sitting and breathing while the bath water ran. Her first act when she stood up was to grasp the doorknob and quietly open the door one inch.

She lit candles. She let one or two drops of hyacinth oil spill into the tub. No bubbles, not this time. Then she disrobed, slowly, looking in the mirror. She did not look away until appreciation of her naked body made her head all the way happy again. When her toe went into the water this was her bath, hers like none before.

This was truly satisfying, this lulling, this sinking while floating, this hot-as-she-wished. She kept it very hot indeed, controlling the taps with curled bare toes. Everything slowed. There was nothing but *here*.

It was so easy to let her hand touch, set free as it was by her acts and courage. And by her awful fucking need. She needed the touching. Her breasts were delicious, her tummy delightful. And waiting for her between her thighs? That which no wine, no chocolate, no money, no shopping, no thing could be as exciting as.

Soon her moans echoed around the tiled bathroom. Heedless, she let everything fly, moaning and cooing and voicing those high little bird cries that felt so good, like pulling the pleasure up to the tops of trees, readying to take flight. Her relentless hand lifted her off and up, up into the thin air until the pressure burst open her person into sparkling shivering shards of sky. The walls of the bathroom fairly shook from the bellow of release.

She sucked in little mewing cries on the way down. She rubbed them in with deft fingers. Her breath was full of deep satisfaction. She thought her face must look very beautiful in that moment. With her lower lip caught slightly in her teeth, she smiled wickedly at the pleasure to be found on earth, hissing the hotness of it into her mouth. And wonderfully spread out before her was a deep pool of thrilling certainty – she could do this to herself as many times as she wished. She could do it again, right now.

The bathroom door opened a few inches. A bottle of wine came in. His hand curled around its neck. Her explosion of laughter was another celebration of earthly pleasure.

"Let the party continue," she crowed, turning on the hot water spigot with her beautiful left foot.

Georgia and Teddy lay exhausted on the bed. They had set a record for their marriage that night, although neither knew it nor cared. They did care about the look of serenity in each other's eyes. She let him see all the way down to the place her huge orgasms came from. *I need you touching me right here*, she prayed to him silently.

"What's in the note?"

She lay on her side facing him on his side.

They were *one thing* at that moment. Her eyes were big and wide and not afraid.

"I love you no matter what. When you are ready, come join me in the pursuit of happiness."

roared off the downslope

April had been away from her lover for six days. That is fact number one.

To end the agony, her automobile raced south on Interstate 15, inbound for Los Angeles. She was about to attain Cajon Pass, considered by Angelenos the beginning of the stretch run. Here the San Andreas Fault had kindly cut a notch in the San Bernardino Mountains, allowing feasible access to the metropolis and basin of eighteen million people below.

April continued her assessment.

Fact two, they had been hot as hell before she left town. There were things she did the night before her departure that made her distrust the evidence of memory. *No, that could not have been me, I don't do that kind of thing.*

Third – she was at a certain point in her monthly cycle. This was a three-day interval out of every twenty-eight when there was no such thing as getting turned on, April was always on, in a constant state of girly heat. A little secret she had masked so far in this affair. *It's just for me*, she justified in her mind, *it twists me happy-dirty.* Well, she was roaring along in the drama of it this very moment.

She glanced at the speedometer. If not for wisdom that California Highway Patrol often lurked on the L.A. side of the pass, she would have dared ninety. Or more. *Come on, come on, take me home, dusty road.*

Last fact: the damned phone sex. Nearly every freakin' night this week from the hotel room in Vegas back to his apartment in Westwood. She had been the crazier in it, once making him hold off until his salacious talk brought on her second climax before she unleashed exact graphic instructions that made him erupt like a berserk King Kong.

She opened the window of the car an inch. Maybe if noise and wind rattled around it would shake her up, disjoint her obsessive daydreams. The air – hot. All it did was bake her brain fully.

Her mind's eye filled with lusty memories. The first time he took her rough from behind. She had asked for him to be more forceful, but then kept edging away. Fed up with her teasing, he threw her on the bed, spread her wide, and moved in like a stallion. The force and power of the first thrust ripping into her body, recalled now, conveyed a hormone burst and white-out in the brain – she slowed the car until the rush subsided.

A montage of other firsts flooded in. First time they did it in public, on the porch of her mother's house. First time she tied him up. That was a good one, because she tortured him with her mouth on his entire body for half an hour until he begged, and no joke about it.

First time his hand snuck beneath her shirt. First time she surprised him with nothing on under. First time she watched his hand stroke it exactly how he wanted it.

First time she felt the tip of his cock slip into her mouth. Oh, damn, she put that image in a loop, vivifying it over and over, imagining the heft and texture of it on her eager lips and tongue. His fucking cock right in her fucking mouth. Oh oh oh.

Then all images began to rage, rushing in rotation, wildly exaggerated, until the briefest flash of his erect cock seemed like grand opera featuring Cupid's mightiest shaft. With each flicker, her brain fired off an inappropriate share of love-dopamine, like a lab rat self-administering too much pleasure juice. April went roaring over the top of Cajon Pass, a love-mobile if ever there was one.

She dropped her hand into her lap. This gesture set off new erotic movies. First time she let him watch her masturbate. First time she put her hand on his and showed him what she liked. First time he made her do it in the car as he drove down the highway. These joined the stream of fevered imagination, escalating the stakes.

She checked her mirrors. She engaged cruise control, setting it just over the speed limit. She shifted her dress up around her waist. *After all, a girl can only take so much*. Her hand slipped under the elastic waistband of the fancy undergarment, triggering remembrance of him doing it. She loved this man getting his hand in her pants. She had let him do it so many times.

She moved her legs apart slightly, as much as was safe, determined to not pull into a rest stop, locked as she was on a beeline to the hive.

With a practiced motion, April's hand fit onto her sex. It went right for home, the perfect little button aching to be set alight. She moaned her happy sorrowful moan right from the first touch. Within seconds, while the car might be descending for landing in L.A., April was accelerating for takeoff.

The images raced on, chasing one another, like a stampeded slide show of her libido. She caressed and tugged and pressed and urged herself on with "oh yes oh yes oh yes oh fucking yes."

She arched back against the seat. The hand did not stop. She turned it a certain way to let thumb rub clit. The other fingers tenderly stroked the inner lips.

As easy as that, fevered as she was, April achieved.

"Ya ah ha oh oh oh ... oh!" She let out the thunder, with no one to hear.

Sailing high, April worked two fingers inside an inch. They pulled the lips of her sex apart. Revealed, exposed, glorious, the writhing insides shuddered fast, splashing delicious juice onto her fingers and thighs.

The way down was gratifyingly long. She kept fingers in. With everything sensitive, slippery touches and caresses caused sweet after-quakes in her thighs.

The slide show in her mind's eye ceased. It was stuck on one image, as if the projector had broken at the decisive frame – the first time he kissed her, at that party, after they had laughed and talked and flirted for hours. That kiss was gentle, sweet, risky, true, with her heart fluttering.

An ironic smile appeared – much as they were sex-mated like tigers ... it had been love first.

April kept one hand in her warm sex for many miles. She roared off the downslope of the mountains, the taste-memory of that first kiss on her lips, homing on the beacon of her waiting lover, making little "oh" sounds often, like Venus surprised by the twang of Cupid's mightiest shaft.

the simple shift of things

He was reflective. She was in the bathroom, busy, he was reflective. He reflected on being paralyzed by stark terror twenty-two months ago, two days before the wedding. It was something that crossed your mind, but until you experience it for real, with wedding rings in your pocket, you don't know what fear is. You are promising that for the rest of your life, perhaps forty, fifty, sixty years, this is the one person you can be in love with and have sex with.

For an honest person committed to monogamy, not holding divorce or 'something on the side' as options, it is extremely scary.

It kept reflecting in his mind that nature had spent millions of years in ferocious, brutal, relentless selection, programming the male animal to spread his seed, achieve maximum fertility for the species through mating with every womb passing by, while also programming the female animal to seek out and accommodate every A-type sperm donor strolling past at her moment of peak fertility. Nature uses potent drugs mainlining directly into the bloodstream to enforce this program.

The odds against monogamy were long.

However, he thought reflectively, perhaps there is hope. Here they were, two years in, and she was getting sexier.

That thought made him impatient. What the hell was taking so long? He really wanted to walk in, but to get her to say 'yes' he had promised to stay out. He put his ear to the bathroom door – sounds in there, things being moved, things being done. He flopped back into bed and pulled the covers over his head.

"Turn out that light," he heard, and popped his head out. "Turn out that light."

"Come on out, I want to see." The bathroom door swung open, but no girl emerged.

"Turn it out."

He reached over and snapped it off. Only moonlight and the general glow of the city lit the room now.

"I feel really, really sexy," she said, standing across the room.

In the faint light he saw her long hair piled up and held by combs. She wore a slinky chemise. Bare feet.

"Let me see."

"Shush," she ordered. "Keep your pants on."

"I'm naked ready to go got no pants now let me see." Testosterone ran through his blood like nitro in a drag racer.

"Shush," she said again. She took a few steps into the room. Hilariously, she seemed ready to bolt out the door, circling toward it, as far away as possible from the bed, never turning her back.

"It's bare," she whispered. "I'm completely bare."

He didn't want to be shushed again, so he just watched from the bed. She moved six feet closer.

"Promise you won't get off the bed."

"Okay."

"I want to show you."

"Okay."

She took the hem of the shift in fingers of both hands and began to lift it delicately. This is a gesture certain to make any man palpitate. His eye followed the uncovering of the line formed by the meeting of thighs as she revealed it inch by inch. This journey led inexorably to the delta of Venus.

The completely nude delta. Not a hair there, anywhere.

She looked down at herself. Then, hem in hands, she looked right in his eyes, laughing quietly, sizzling with excitement.

"Oh, it's creamy and delicious," he said. "I want to kiss it for an hour."

She squealed, yanking down the chemise, vibrating in an animated dance, stomping bare feet, turning in place. He turned the light back on and watched with fascination, amused and aroused by her ingenuous modesty as it wobbled off the wagon. She calmed, but kept the garment pulled down in exaggerated tenacity, as if to prevent some miscreant wind or randy boyfriend from lifting the hem above the radioactive zone.

"I changed my mind," she said.

"Right."

"Rewind."

There was a beat of time.

"Show me again," he whispered.

She froze in place. He could sense her not breathing. Then she turned to face him straight on and took two steps closer. Her hands relaxed, the better to be graceful, and she slowly raised the curtain – not smiling now.

"It's fantastic," he said, eyes riveted on the vee.

"I want to open my legs and let you see everything."

"Not yet."

"Okay." Her voice changed direction, became languorous. "Look at it as long as you want."

"That's why I asked for this. To see."

"I know."

"I think it's beautiful."

"It's so bare."

"Really bare."

"I mean, it's just radical shaving, millions of girls do it, no big deal, but I've never. Ever."

"Do you like holding the nightie up like that

for me to see?"

She nodded.

"Turn around and walk over there."

He was rewarded with a splendid view of her rounded backside in motion for five or six steps. She walked back, slowly. He savored the usual sway of hips and pelvis, but now also the simple shift of things on the curve of her mons veneris and the cleft running down from it. The lips moved in opposing directions ever so slightly with each footfall, as if kissing each other with salacious affection. That must have been going on all this time!

Pulling up with crossed hands, she turned the chemise inside out, lifting it up and off her body. It went flying across the room. He slid off the bed and approached.

"I'm your naked girlfriend," she whispered.

They embraced. Hunger rose from skin on skin. Naked on naked. Body to body. This is what the sense of touch is for. Inflammation of mates. Adoring. Sex.

His cock went hard as a rock. As a writer, he would never write that. Never. A lame cliché. He could feel the organ asserting itself against her belly and knew she liked it.

"... hard as a rock," she said.

Her breasts pressed his chest. The kiss they lit off blossomed into something giant and roaring. She kissed as hard and deep as he, fighting his lips and tongue, sucking them and wetting them with hers. Completely swamping his mind, a vast urgency to get her new nakedness wide open.

She yanked herself away, stumbling slightly as she wiggled free. Her face shone bright, full of daring.

"Now can I show you?"

"Yes."

She drifted to the side of the bed, not looking at him. She rested her bottom on it, then drew her feet up and put her arms around her knees, all contained and nicely folded, pausing for effect. He took two steps to reach the bed, cock hard, jutting, and swaying.

She looked deliberately at the erection with appetite. "That is so beautiful. I'm sick for cock right now."

"Yes."

"I want it splitting me open right where I'm bare. I'm all wet from being so naughty and bare and all."

"It's wet?"

She latched onto that, looked up at him demurely, arms still folded around closed legs. "I'm squeezing and I can feel the insides slippery. I want something to ram in, bad."

"Open your legs and let me see."

"Only if you put your fingers in, get them wet, then spread it on me, like healing cream after shaving."

That was outrageous. Where was his shy girl? Sitting forlorn in the bathroom.

"Open your legs."

She did it in slow motion, with every bit of heat he could have wanted, everything between so magnificently free and naked, his mate of two years now his new lover.

Then, legs apart like wings, she made him fall in carnal love all over again, stroking with her hand, showing him her fingers shiny, using them to expose the lips, the underlips, the inside mysteries, the crowning summit of the clit, majestic in its dominance, if a little lonely without a forest at its feet. A woman caressing her sex with gentle pleasure – it puts a lump in a man's throat to watch.

He touched the lips with two fingers, spread them, and slid in. Drawing warm juice out, he made the newly shaven area wet, balming it, treasuring it.

When he looked in her eyes, she said it again: "I'm your naked girlfriend."

She turned on the bed onto all fours and asked to be touched from behind, keeping her legs far apart to give access, watching over her shoulder, letting him caress with no other agenda indefinitely – only to pleasure with sensitive hands forever. Swaying her hips to his rhythms, she began to moan. His fingers at her clit and inside the soaked cave incited, thrilled unmercifully, and caused the moaning. She raised her bottom even more, to offer better. Near tears, she whispered to him.

"I'm so naked. So open it hurts. Hurt me more sweet."

How beautiful her exposure – he felt it in his chest – his caresses now more tender than ever, because she placed her sexual self, her living yoni, in his care.

"Take it. Get me naked every day, get me wide open like this, touch me all the way in, all the way to my heart."

"Oh my God."

"Put it in now, please put your cock in. Turn me over and fuck me."

They joined. He thrust magnificently, deep right away. A difference – no hair, there, a psychic protection stripped away. The erotic was close-in now. The illusion of more room. The tight way she gripped his cock, greater than before. Each stroke thudded solid, staying deep an extra half-second, rubbing his pubic bone against hers, pressing the unprotected clit, inflaming her mightily.

"Right in, right in, right there, right there, there, there. Oh holy fuck, there."

Most exposed – her eyes. She opened them wide ... and surrendered everything. At the very top, no scream as her joy erupted. Only a prayerful whisper spilling from her throat.

"Love me."

They had dared for fun. A little thing. Only this small change. Now they lay tangled in each other's arms, breathing hard, awash in the glow of something big filling the bed. A tiny risk that blew up huge, to knock their married mating sideways.

They could do that for sixty years.

In a stunning flash, a challenge rushed in. He stopped breathing. *If I were bare, there, how much closer could we be?*

too bright to believe in

After their first weekend as lovers, he realized noise might be a problem. He noticed stares in the parking lot Monday morning. No one said anything, but he knew. And looming large in the equation – the awareness that even at current decibel levels, she was holding back.

"I can't help it," she said, laughing, blushing, breathless, in the middle of last night. How many times on the way up had she begged, 'Make me scream?'

So infatuated was he, so jazzed to be tangling with this wild woman, the noise served as a point of fire, a spur to excitement. Dangerously, he wanted more, to send her rocketing beyond orbit, half wishing the police would come knocking on the door.

We might have to be those obnoxious L.A. punks who don't give a damn about anyone else's peace and quiet.

Then, he got an idea.

In March every year, a two-week window opens on spring in the Mohave Desert. The jumping-off date is determined by winter storms swirling into California from the vast Pacific Ocean, driven sufficiently south to lift themselves over the San Gabriel and San Bernardino Mountains. The elevating clouds race over the crestline down into the wide bowl that was once a sea and spill themselves onto the parched rocks and dust. These few storms carry the only water the Mohave will enjoy all year, their number can be counted on one hand, and they bring outrageous flowers.

He took her out to the desert. He targeted an area he knew well, familiarized during his days in the Marines half a decade ago.

First, however, they spent a great night in Palm Springs. Her crazy-in-bed business did not relent in hotel rooms, apparently. It occurred to him that their neighbors above, below, and especially on the other side of the wall against which their bed abutted, must have enjoyed a fascinating hour around midnight.

Now, the next day, he was glad to be driving an off-road-capable SUV. Time to take this wildcat off road, all right. Give her room to growl.

Just past the town of Twenty-Nine Palms on California 62, he slowed to take a left turn onto a dirt way that was barely there. He knew it would deteriorate even further in a mile.

"This is it," he said.

"This is what, where's the road?" she said, with a little real nervousness.

"We're going over that rise," he said, pointing to a low ridge a mile to the north. "Beyond that is my secret spot."

"I'm ready for some trees or something. I don't think I'm really going to be a desert person. Don't be angry, but it's just brown and rocky and all these shrubs."

"It's okay."

"You like it, though?"

"I like the wide-open space and the way it gets quiet at night."

"You've been out here at night?"

"Dozens of times. I was stationed at a base a few miles away to the west. We were in the desert at night all the time."

"Jeez."

As they ascended the gentle slope, he related one or two stories of his time in the Marines. Also, he spoke about the conditions that bring the flowers here, how the spring explosion was always short-lived, completely absent some years, fine many others, and utterly outrageous perhaps one year in ten.

"You have to catch it just right."

She made a joke about Marines and flowers, but it was respectful enough. She was intimidated by him, he realized. *Maybe this will work, maybe not.*

They topped the rise and stopped.

"Oh my God," she shouted, jumping out.

"Bingo."

Spread out before them, blanketing the partial bowl between here and the next height, a vast sea of colors assaulted the senses, yellow mostly, but shot through with purple, orange, and lavender. In places, a pale green glow seemed to appear if a breeze blew for a moment. After five minutes of admiration for the display, they climbed back into the vehicle. Within twenty minutes he had driven around the perimeter of this and two other hollows, each more spectacular in bloom than the next, wound through the edge of a field of nearly iridescent orange, and came down into a wash where all the colors vied for ascendancy in a riotous mélange. The stems were tall. This had to be the spot it rained most.

They were far, far off-road, miles from any other living soul.

After an interval of talking and walking in the flowers, plus wine, she turned on him and unbuttoned his shirt. She could kiss as if dying of thirst, and he did not mind one bit. She kissed the shirt right off him.

"Take my shirt off me now," she said.

"Wait." He pulled down the tailgate of the SUV and moved away a cooler. Yanking aside a car blanket, he revealed the floor to be conveniently fitted with a comfortable mattress and cotton bedding, pillows and all. Her eyes got big. She giggled.

"What, not out here on the ground in the flowers?" He regarded her there, ten feet away, thigh-deep in a sea of *oenothera biennis*, bright yellow as the sun.

"In here, where the thread count is two-hundred fifty."

"Can we leave the tailgate down? I want to see these flowers while we do it."

He went and got her. Lifted the shirt right off her back. Soon they were both naked, surrounded by discarded jeans and boots. He made her walk ahead, so he could admire her shape. With a whoop, she jumped into their makeshift bower.

He put her to the test, there in the blooming and fecund Mohave Desert springtime. And why not – she insisted on outlandish behavior in his bed, why not get to the bottom of it.

"Don't hold anything back," he said. She giggled nervously at that. "Seriously. Go for it. All the way."

They fought to be best at open-mouth kissing. Even if he won, he would never admit it. Soon, he eased down her body.

"Oh, yes," she murmured, "once again to fall in love with your mouth." He displayed no reservations in its use. The final target was unguarded and openly displayed, to say the least. And wet. Perfect for the pleasures devoutly to be wished – the taste of woman.

He would not let her explode right away. With the first proximity of coming, he swiveled to have her take his erection in her mouth, letting up the devouring of her ripe sex for a moment. Reversing back, each time she approached climax, he switched the caress and position, causing a retreat and regroup.

A golden glow reflected inside their space from rays of the sun glancing off ten thousand blossoms. He liked the way it shone on them in the act.

Three times he returned his mouth to her favorite spot. He knew it to be her favorite, because the joy-screams erupted when his lips covered it.

"Oh oh oh oh oh. Yes. Please. Yes. Please. Oh oh oh oh oh."

He opened her with his mouth and sought the deep flesh.

"Don't stop don't stop don't stop. Make me come. So fucking good, right there. Right there, make me come. Eat me. Make me come."

She swayed hips off the mattress and wiggled herself as deep as possible against him, gathering great scoops of air and releasing them, moaning and bellowing like some mammal long extinct, a giant one.

"Oh my God," she began to bellow. "Ohmygod, ohmygod."

Her movements grew desperate, but never enough to threaten the sure connection between her wide-open sex and his mouth.

Then, her voice shifted down. Every gulping breath came faster and bigger, releasing a low, solid wall of sound, the last note of which was long, surreal, throbbing out from the gut's gut. She took one more gigantic breath, and it caught – she was falling. Her voice went silent and her body rigid. He spread the lips apart with his mouth, put everything into two, three, four voluptuous kisses slipped all over the lips, the inside flesh, and raw clit-bud. Frozen, she was utterly defenseless against the intimacy and open lust of those kisses. They were devastating.

She fell. The bottom of the abyss loomed up. How else to explain the shattering, roaring scream that erupted from her shaking body, rolling out over the expanse of the desert. She screamed again and again.

She survived her fall, of course. Her breath, her body unfroze. The deep source of her sex liquids let loose. Her womb shuddered with convulsion after convulsion – he could feel them, holding his lip against her clit with his tongue reaching inside.

He did not move his mouth from her soaring yoni. Her hand found his and they interwove at the side of her hip. The sounds of her, the scent and taste of her, the warmth of her flesh in his mouth, and the golden glow all around them – all these earthy things seemed true, but in another world.

He came to lie beside her, searching her face. She continued to breathe hard, staring at him with wide eyes. Many parts of her twitched with no control – a full-body orgasm. He let her coast down, a descent that took long minutes while the yellow flowers waved in the sun, too bright to believe in, nearly. Eventually, a great sigh escaped her settling body, and he felt the end arrive.

"I want to die like that, someday," she said.

"That was amazing."

Her eyes closed.

"You're not freaked out?" she asked

"No."

"I'm afraid of it, but I can't stay away from it either."

"What?"

She opened her eyes. "All the power."

He held steady.

"You're not freaked out?"

He shook his head.

"I've scared away every other man I've been with."

That thought hung in the air. He had seen her after-serenity many times over the past two weeks, but the depth this time was profound. Something vigilant had gone limpid with abandon.

He spoke.

"If I hang around, would you promise to find out everything you know about it and talk to me?"

Her eyes filled with tears. "There might be a lot."

"We'll have to figure out a way to keep my landlord from evicting me for disturbing domestic tranquility," he said, smiling wryly at her, moving his body on top, separating her thighs with his.

She burst out laughing and blushed right down to the tips of her naked breasts.

sorrowful

escalation
the scent they had made
sentiments of return

escalation

Kai clicked off without leaving a voice mail. Her pessimism knew he had listened to four prior ones she left over the past three days – with no response.

"No more voice mails. His phone'll tell him he missed my call," she said, placing hers on the counter by her wine glass. "That's my escalation."

Her friend watched warily from the other side of the counter. Jeanie had confirmed he was not dead, drunk, or demented. She had spotted him at lunch this afternoon outside his office, laughing and talking to a buddy.

"Not the first time for this," said Jeanie.

"No. Third time in the four months we've been dating."

"Kai, how long are you going to keep giving him a break?"

"Maybe it's my fault."

"No."

"Maybe it is."

"You have to break it off."

"Wait wait wait."

"End it."

Kai closed her eyes. She held up a finger to tell her friend to suspend, took two deep breaths, covered her face with both hands, scrubbed away the stress, and let out a guttural scream.

She turned away, to tell the truth. "It's probably over."

"Probably?"

Kai paused. Looking back to her friend, she blinked, twice. "Yes."

"What did you do to him?" asked Jeanie.

"Not a damn thing."

"Really."

"We had that date three nights ago ..."

"I'm completely aware that that was more than a date," said Jeanie.

"It was a date."

"No, remember, you were going for more. You pretended you were joking, but you told me, "... think I'll turn tonight into a honeymoon'."

"I didn't say that."

"You said it, Kai, and you had an agenda in your eyes. Now tell me what you did to him."

"You don't need the dirty details, do you?"

"Ah, yeah girl, you've been ghosted. If you want to figure this out, you have to tell me what you did. Now tell me."

Kai took a deep breath that included a re-up for her friend being a true friend. To be trusted.

"Something happened during sex."

"Ah-ha."

"He's good in bed."

"What you mean good?" Jeanie made big eyes.

"Jean."

"Okay, okay."

"Did you ever have a guy who did it so strong, made you scream and shake, made you hold your breath waiting for him all the next day with your pelvis screaming, until he came busting in and threw you on the bed and didn't stop until you exploded three times?"

"Whoa."

"And then jumps out of bed right after? Starts plotting to leave the apartment?"

"Oh."

"The other night, I wrapped my arms and legs around him and wouldn't let him up."

Jeanie nodded and crossed her arms around her torso. "Then what?"

"We were both still breathing hard. My legs were shaking, but I said, 'can we make love now'?"

"Oh my God."

"It just popped out of my brain."

"Then what?"

"He didn't get angry. He didn't run. But he froze. Right there on top of me. I whispered to him ... he can do it twice in a row, sometimes ... I said 'put it in again, slow. Love me with it, tender, and don't take your eyes away from mine'."

"You asked for full eye-contact slow sex?"

"Yes."

"All the way to the end?"

"Yes."

"What happened?"

"He couldn't. Wouldn't. Didn't. I let it go. He walked out five minutes later."

Both women pictured the emotional landscape. Each took a draught of wine. Then Jeanie turned the truth on her friend.

"Most men can't do that, even on a honeymoon. Maybe never. Some women, neither."

"I need it, Jeanie. Not just during sex. I need to see his soul with no defenses up, lots of times."

A beat of time. A pregnant pause. Then Jean's psychic water broke.

"How soon after you break up can I have him?"

They burst into brilliant laughter that snapped the tension.

Kai's cell chimed in. It was the ring tone for him. The two friends looked at each other for guts. Kai shook her head no, with wet eyes.

"You're done?"

Kai nodded – and let something die.

"I'm not going to do the dumping, but let me pick up."

"Okay."

"Kai's phone ... no, I can't interrupt her ... she's writing in her journal ... no, I won't ... because she asked me to answer her phone if you called ... no, she didn't tell me what's going on ... yeah, I know something's going on all right, she broke a few dishes tonight on purpose ... what the fuck did you do to her? ... nothing? ... nothing, really? ... I'm going to hang up now, call back, I won't answer ... leave a voice mail, and you'd better be really good at begging."

the scent they had made

"Marriage is dead," she said. "Long live marriage."

His head snapped around. "What the hell are you talking about?"

"I'm not sure yet. A woman in my new story simply came right out and said it. It'll probably be a few days until I know what she means."

He was accustomed to such mysteries, when one of her characters simply 'shows up' or 'does something unexplainable' and it's all perfectly natural for her to be as much in the dark as the next person about it. He made the mistake once of asking why she was not all knowing, not in control of her writing. She had scolded him severely, and it was weeks before she began to fill him in on current developments as soon as they cropped up. He was wary now at all like occurrences.

"Is she married?" he asked, an eccentric move in tense chess.

"No. She's just talking with someone who interests her. I think she's testing him."

"Which are you pulling for, 'is dead' or 'long live'?"

She gave him a curious glance as if admiring the question itself. They were on the way out of the apartment.

"It's not up to me," she said slowly, "it's up to the characters, I've told you that a thousand times."

"Right. Just because a character says something or does something, it doesn't mean you believe in it."

"Right."

"But can't you root for one side or the other?" he asked.

She glanced at him again, then wordlessly began applying lipstick with attitude, head angled toward the reflective brass plate above the elevator button, which he pressed.

He believed he had sacrificed a pawn yet gained enough position to fare well in the endgame. The elevator opened downstairs as if freezing the board for the night. They sailed briskly through the building's lobby fronting Ninth Street. As usual, there were no empty cabs rushing along toward Sixth Avenue. They turned as one and jumped out, heading for the big avenue, ready for a night at play in the city.

He was intensely grateful for the taxi and its competent driver. The rain pelted it relentlessly. She was chilled, he could tell, by tension in her arms where his wrapped around, snugging her up close.

"Almost home."

She nodded, hair moving against his shoulder. He launched a rant.

"I still can't get over DeLeon actually getting a promotion at that stupid company. He hates that job. He's useless already, now it'll be a total joke, with a higher salary. It's like a comedy of the absurd. Bizarro world. They should kick him out. No, he should kick them out, but now he's going up the damn ladder. Unbelievable."

"Peter Principle," she said with little enthusiasm.

"Maybe if they give him something really repulsive, he'll hate it so much he can make vice-president in another year. And Rai is just dandy with it. Wife of Mister up-the-down-staircase."

"You're trying to make me smile," she said quietly.

"Well, you remember in 'Up the Down Staircase' when Sandy Dennis makes this long pitch for her class of hooligans to quiet down just once so she can at least try to teach and finally they all shut up for once but it's a trick they're really just holding their breath in a conspiracy to play with her head and she's surprised but she decides to go for Emily Dickinson and turns around to the board and writes 'There is no frigate like a book ...' and they all explode in a riot."

"Frig it," she said disconsolately.

"Frigate," he said.

The rain had begun while they were at dinner with friends two hours ago. Their table provided a view of the engulfed street. During the first course, they commented on the downpour. Good New Yorkers all, they toted sturdy umbrellas, but a change in plan was seriously considered, since now cabs could no longer be taken for granted. It was during the discussion of how to follow them down to the Village that Donna dropped a bomb, announcing that two of their circle would not be meeting them at the destination as planned, and the reason was not the weather, but rather – they had broken up.

Now their cab deposited them right at the curb, so they could scuffle out and under the edge of the apartment's bad-weather canopy extension. They rode up to the seventh floor.

While they changed into bedtime clothes and fussed, he stopped trying to make conversation. He had gotten her home, at least.

She came out of the bathroom with her hair pulled back into a severe ponytail, having ruthlessly scrubbed her face bare. Her outfit reflected a quest for warmth – a full thermal cotton body suit, a sweatshirt over it that said, 'Property of NYU Mens Ski Team,' and white thigh-high legwarmers all the way down to thick green socks. He was respectful of her mood, he really was, but she looked so damn adorable, he cracked up in a moment she wasn't looking.

He watched her traverse into the kitchen and open the refrigerator on a mission for a glass of juice. When she returned, she lifted her sober face to him.

"Cindy and Jeremy. You think they really broke up?"

"Uh-huh," he replied. "Portia told me while we were getting coats that Cindy has left town, no one knows where she is. I'm surprised you didn't ask Portia for more details."

"I'm a little freaked out."

"Because of the story ..."

"Because of that stupid line about marriage is dead, and then I hear this. They were hip deep in the wedding, for God's sake."

She was quiet for a moment. Then a look he had never seen came over her.

"Get me warm under the covers and hold me for a long time. Then make love." She took his hand and walked them into the bedroom. "I want you inside me."

He searched her face for weakness that might accompany such a request. There was none. It was as if watching a good soldier nearing the front line. His heart ached with sympathy for her. He knew Cindy had asked her to help with the wedding dress, that she had been part of that, the dress and what had been making her friend a bride. And now Cindy was dumped practically at the altar and had run away without a word.

During the night, they took comfort in the big bed. It rained, with only a brief respite or two. He stroked her hair. He kissed her many times. He never took his touch away. She cried, finally, opening her heart. Cindy had been very vulnerable, she said. Cindy had been playing for all the marbles.

He kept his arms around her. She pressed her body back against him when they were like spoons. Deep in the night she put her hand on his sex, held it like a treasure.

"I love it in my hand," she said. "It's hard and it wants me."

"Yes," he said.

She turned to look in his eyes. "You want me."

"Yes," he said. "But not just that." He paused for a moment to get it right. In the circumstances she deserved assurances, having earned them through countless instances of trusting him, yet he deserved to be unbeholden to irrational insecurities in her. In quiet peace, he tapped the reservoirs of confidence between such extremes, strengths built over years. He spoke from that center.

"I'll never leave you."

Under their down comforter and across their

marriage bed, they made love with steady desire, taking turns on top. They held each other's gaze as far into the moment of overflow as nature would allow. Into the utter silence of a break in the rain, when he could not restrain his own tears for how much each had given the other this night, she said the sexiest thing of all.

"I believe you."

Gray light seeped through the last of the rain. Dawn. He awoke to stillness in the apartment. She was not in the bed. Then he heard typing in the other room. He pulled the comforter around his naked body and inhaled the scent they had made in the night. He went back to sleep at once.

the sentiments of return

An exceptional hotel room in Edgartown notwithstanding, she sought primitive places as true luxury.

Along a path jutting from Lambert's Cove Road, for instance, she discovered a dell choked with ancient scrub oaks, trunks and limbs contorted by the elements. A silent hour walking in this strange wood wrought an effusion of loneliness, and from it allowed an aching tinge of loss to well up, to linger, to diminish, finally.

Then, hiking at the outermost edge of land east on Chappaquiddick, she created solitude by secreting behind a dune to avoid the occasional fisherman's buggy racing to Wasque. The sea pounded there. Its thrumming loosed more feelings. She lay prone in the sand, alternately ecstatic from the sun and indulgent with melancholy. That was luxurious. At dusk, she ran into the surf and washed ragged memory away.

These forays were warm-ups. She headed up-Island on the third morning, a slow ride with the Jeep open to the sky. Each new vista stirred remembrance of her original summer here, in tranquil places with quaint old names.

"You can't say this isn't spectacular."
"It's unbelievable," she replied as they passed through a picture-perfect tiny village and emerged into a forested stretch.
"We don't cut down big trees here."
"Obviously."
The magic of the place was on her. At West Tisbury, they curved around a turn to the juncture of several other roads. The granddaddy of oaks stood there, ludicrously spectacular.
"That's as big as they get on Martha's Vineyard. I've always liked that tree, like it's the king of all the others."
"And I have a boyfriend who notices things like that," she said with fateful astonishment.

At Aquinnah, she found a place to park, good all day. The weather promoted her mood, strong sun, high sky, cool breeze – with a squall skirting the horizon at the edge of the sea. Summer approached, yet today no multitudes threatened her quest for solitude, not the madness of high season yet. Thus, her small knapsack, her hiking shoes, her layers of shirts for shedding when it warmed – nothing would deny her will, the need to reach the most important lonely luxury spot of all.

With the first step away from the car, reverie blossomed. She scrambled down the slope to gain the narrow beach, already half transported twenty-seven years back, recalling the day he had shown her this very path from cliff to shore. When she turned left to follow the high tide line, sun and wind resplendent on the Atlantic wave tops, the sentiments of return dominated. She allowed a delicious illusion into existence, him taking his place, walking by her side.

"This beach is so open and free."
"Yes," he said.
"And the wind ..."
"Yes."
She stopped, shook her head in the keen breeze, deliberately letting her hair run wild, then gathered it into one handful and secured it with a band. There was a moment when the walk should have resumed down the shore. She held him, instead, with her eyes.
"Where are we going in this empty place?"
He paused. The words hung between them, gathering portent.
"Let me show you," he said.
He took her hand and led the way up a dune directly ahead. The scene at the top was so ideal she could scarcely credit it. Gazing right, the Atlantic shoreline marched on easterly, a hem on the

sparkling restless sea. It appeared to not vary for tens of miles. Ahead and to their left lay a shapely lake divided from the ocean by only a narrow barrier beach. The lake extended inland, surrounded by dunes or brush-covered banks, giving way to marshy inlets on the far side, water birds rising to the sky above its rippling surface and long bending reeds. A few structures stood at the lakefront, and the corner of a village could be glimpsed between two hilltops far beyond the thither shore. A separate small pool, Lily Pond, lay at their feet.

"Do you see that rise at the corner of the lake by the sea?" he asked.

"Yes. The house just up from the shore?"

"That's it. Everything from there to the right and going down to the ocean, that's all on the property."

"Fantastic. I can hardly believe it, it's like a movie. What is this lake?"

She awaited the reply, savoring the bright day.

"Squibnocket Pond," he said.

She reached the boundary of the property at the ocean's edge. Turning left and inland, climbing up, she found the path. Another shock of memory – down this way she had run, young, exultant, naked, to plunge into the ocean twenty-seven years ago.

She kept on. Shrubs and stunted oaks closed in on the path. She wound through as they became taller. Then, fifteen yards along, she stepped into a clearing. The revivification of that time slammed all the way home.

The cabin still survived, barely. It canted up from the sand, ramshackle and storm-damaged, obviously abandoned. A miniature dune had blown up against it, its small porch collapsed, front door gone missing. Numerous planks and shakes lay strewn about, half buried in the sand. Her heart ached at the beautiful loss, again the loss.

And an astonishing development, something new to this spot. Rampant everywhere, blocking the windows, filling half the small yard, a rambling, dense blackberry bramble, laden with fruit, stood guard over the dying beach cabin, the place of her first time.

"Stop!"

"I want to make you scream again."

"Stop you maniac, stop, I can't take any more." *She laughed, trying to roll away from his relentless touch.*

She managed to sit up, drawing his face close with hands on either side of his head to gain a fragment of control, and lit off a kiss, taking his mouth in hers. The taste of sex was in it. She took the lead, skidding her lips along the inside of his, tip of tongue following. When the kiss swelled with sweet liquid, she swam in helpless pleasure, cooing gently, shuddering.

They broke apart, laughing, moaning in mock overload.

"That's outrageous," he said

"Your mouth should be against the law," she joked.

"I'm not guilty."

"Really?"

"Okay, I am guilty."

"That would make it so sexy, if it were against the law," she said.

"Listen, my father is a Selectman of Chilmark. We could get an ordinance passed."

"What, no French kissing on Martha's Vineyard?"

"No intimate kissing of any kind. It is forbidden. You can't take down a stone wall, you can't cut down old oaks, you can't paint your trim anything but white, and you can't kiss a girl until she begs for mercy."

They laughed, smirky and knowing. Then their voices trailed away as if drowned by waves as the sound of the sea filled the cabin. She froze, eyes wide open, holding her breath.

Then, one slow blink, a sigh, and she tilted over gently to lay her body, prone, naked, offered, next to her first lover. When his eyes reached hers, after caressing up from her parted thighs, she whispered.

"Again."

Standing by the ruined shanty, with the bramble all around, she revived that day. Oh, they had been blind with immortality. She could feel the edges of it now, the surety they had stayed time with their souls, that even if duration were blatantly marked by the ineluctable rhythm of wave after wave falling on the shore, the power of opening each other to bursting could yet stop time.

This exact reality returned to her now in full. She took it on her soul, unprotected. She let it run and measured the impotence of the surf's sound against it once again, as when young, lingering as daylight waned, not wanting to release everything back to the sea.

She stayed in the clearing next to the ruined cabin until loss finished in her this way.

"Where are the berries?"
"I don't know."
"Get them."
"I've already eaten too many, you get them."
She rose and padded across to a tiny table near the open door. With deliberate intention, she filled the door frame, backlit from the westering sun. She arched her back. She knew all he could see was her shape, soft belly and hips, and especially the lifted and offered curve of sweet breasts. Slowly, one hand rose to her mouth and dropped a blackberry in.

That's all it took. He leapt from the bed. With an exaggerated squeal, she smashed open the screen door and bolted across the cabin yard. Looking behind, she tossed the remaining stock of summer berries at him in a wild arch, missing, launching them into the undergrowth. Ecstatic with the thrill of being so fucking alive, she turned and raced down the path to the crashing sea.

ecstatic

until my lips are sweet
aching and naked
above the canyon
where only joy was
wanting her scent close
its wildest beast
girl in love
see in
how quiet you can be
the call of the great beasts
love in bed

until my lips are sweet

"No."

That stopped his hand.

Oh, she craved the attempts, the intrusion of strong fingers under her skirt, the persistence to push her thighs apart, yes, this a woman craves from the man to whom she is given. And whom she possesses.

But now she folded up and twisted away, taking refuge in the corner of the car.

"No."

His breathing raced in neutral. No back-off in intent in his face. She liked that. *Keep trying,* was in her eyes.

"Let me in ..."

"No."

"Kissing, that's it?"

"You agreed, only kissing."

"Cancel it."

"No."

She liked holding the line. They would drive to their house by the lake where resistance would vanish like fog on Sunday.

Thrilling, holding him off for play. During the drive, she had enticed with subtle bends of the torso and smiles of insincere modesty flashed with no shame. Inflamed by her ripe presence and come-hither glances, he jerked the car onto a side lane. She set the limit at kissing. He agreed – a miscalculation of her oral deviltry. Now he could not stick to the rules. She could hear him thinking – *resume kissing only, or put his hand under the skirt against the rules, or drive?*

Torture.

Her courage rose, buoyed by a challenge of risking he had dropped into the conversation earlier, across a slate tabletop with two wine glasses waiting.

"I have a dare," she said.

"What is it?"

"Put your power away in this car and I'll make the kissing hot. Hotter. Hottest."

"What?"

"Stop trying. If you stop, I'll do something hot."

"What?"

"I'm turning off my defenses. If you try for me again, I won't resist, I'll surrender. I'll beg you to take me, right here in this car. We'll climb in the back seat, so you can get leverage, so you can ravage me good."

"Ravage?"

"Yes. Ravage me, destroy me with your member, devastate me with your proud manhood. In the back seat of a car."

He didn't laugh.

"But you'll miss out on my secret. It's scary for me. I don't know when I'll have the nerve to do it again."

A frown tightened his brow, as if she were trying to take away his rights or something. Then the brow smoothed.

"Okay," he whispered.

With shields down, she came out of her corner, unwinding and flowing across the seat, tilting her head to give her mouth. He took it with a moan in his throat.

Behind closed eyelids, the kiss erupted. His lips and tongue roamed with authority. He circled, licking the inside of her cheeks, forcing his lips under her tongue, sucking her liquids into his mouth. Then, he sank deeper. She understood – to dominate an orifice not denied. Her throat and jaw relaxed to let him. A carnal prayer rose in her imagination.

Make me pay.

Her mouth flooded with wet kisses turned to syrup. He put more in, mercilessly. She held the back of her mouth closed, not wanting to swallow a drop. He stirred the juices, roamed the flesh inside, marking it, drinking it.

She had never taken a kiss this extreme, never

in all their time, never since she gave herself into his eroticism the day they mated for love for good.

A whimper escaped, and a shudder through her body. She backed out. She looked deep in his eyes and swallowed, then parted lips so he could see in.

"All gone. I drank the wet kiss. All gone."

"More," he said, moving in.

"Wait. I have a better way. Here comes my part of the dare."

She moved out of his arms to the window on her side of the car. Glancing at him once, she put her fingers at the hem of her skirt and drew it up above the waist, revealing bare legs and a white something tucked into the delta. A corner of her mind sensed the provocation, knew he might charge in – she would not set vigilance against it, would not resist if he lunged.

She put her fingers in the waistband of the garment and slid it down to her ankles. Revealed in the dim light, the tempting wavy line, topped by a tiny bud. Her hand covered the vee. Thighs parted. Two fingers disappeared.

Then, gracefully, the hand lifted away and turned in the moonlight. They saw wetness glimmering. She moved the fingers to the lips of her mouth, brushing across them until liquids transferred. Her lips glistened.

She turned to show him.

"Don't kiss me yet," she said. "I want to make

my mouth wetter. More juice until my lips are sweet."

This time she didn't look down, holding his gaze instead. When the hand returned to her face, she gave out little sounds of arousal as the wetness transferred to her lips. She moved separated fingers around her face, touching here and there.

"I love the smell of it," she said, a whisper in the night. "I'll make myself wet this way as many times as you want. Lick me and kiss me." She leaned forward, parted her lips, and offered her perfumed mouth with heartbreaking tenderness.

To her joy, they touch-kissed only, brushing mouths, inhaling. With lips barely parted, fitting and pressing lightly, tiny strings of wetness – her sex wetness – bridged between them each time they lifted off. Once or twice, the tip of his tongue emerged to taste.

"You like this way of making my lips wet, don't you?" she whispered to him.

"You'd kiss your sex if you could reach it."

"Yes, I would," she said. "I'd lick it and drink it for hours."

Three times she renewed the wetness from the source below, each time with more abandon. With the last, with most of her face wet, he roamed everywhere, inhaling, tasting. Finally, he opened her mouth with his and pulled the scent inside, under her tongue, and along the inside of lips. She remained deeply surrendered, and would have taken another of those fat kisses, far, far into her mouth, felt herself offering the back of her throat for it.

Instead, he pulled away.

"How am I doing?" he asked.

"Fantastic," she said.

"We're going home now. It'll take half an hour."

She put her hand between her thighs.

"Drive fast," she said.

aching and naked

"Think you've got it?"

"Yes."

"Repeat it back to me."

"You'll be seated at eight. I'll be your waiter. You'll say to go slow. At the end she'll want dessert, you'll put up a fight against it, but then you'll give in."

"Right."

"You'll order two slices of the gâteau au chocolat, but I'll bring just one to the table and say it's the last one. Instead of serving it to her, I'm supposed to put it down for you. You'll take a bite right away."

"Yes."

"Then I'm supposed to run away and keep everyone away from your table."

"Yes."

"There'll be trouble over the chocolate."

"Yes."

"Okay, I've got it," said the waiter.

"You have my charge card number. Put the dinner on it. I'll slip your tip to you in cash when you serve the gâteau."

"Okay, Mr. Pell."

The waiter waited. He should have walked away, but instead he waited. Then he asked.

"Mr. Pell, it's none of my business, I guess, but would you be willing to tell me what you're going to say tonight? Your punchline? The whole thing's leading up to some big question or announcement, right? When she gets mad you have the chocolate?"

"Sorry. Private."

Seeing the look on the waiter's face, he took pity.

"Are you trying to figure out how to say something to someone?"

"Yes."

"Keep your breathing steady. Realize you're playing for all the marbles. Reach in for the most dangerous thing in your gut. No more than seven words. Risk everything."

Mr. Pell played it well, early that evening, by taking charge. At first, she resisted, claiming it was her turn to run everything, then gave herself into his control when he uttered a certain promise in her ear. He made up the game. The rules. He began giving intimate orders, which were obeyed. He teased in the shower, touching without letting her touch, her hands raised high above her head in imaginary bondage. He ordered her to let him kiss without her kissing back and made her shudder from tenderness in his hands on her undefended ribcage.

The exquisite arc to full bloom required perhaps ten minutes of touching after the shower. Then, he was in. A stroke. Another. Then out, all the way out, that sweet hollow feeling of loss, yes, that ripe male sadness when withdrawing unexpended, a melancholy women do not understand.

Now he lay his organ against the orifice – not in – slipping against lips with the underside of his cock.

"Rub me," she said, voice thick.

"Don't tell me what to do."

"Rub me."

"Quiet."

Her head fell back. Her arms circled his neck, legs cinching tight around his waist. Her bottom rested on the dressing table, just on its edge. He stood planted solid in front of her.

"Please please please. Oh please, in."

Ignoring.

He passed his hands under her thighs, circled around to the mouth between, put fingers in place on the lips, pulled them apart and pinned them back, laying open the tender flesh. Then he renewed his slithering attack. His organ slipped along the lips and pressed against the glans each

love in bed

time.

"Rub me..."

"What did you say?"

"Rub me. Rub me rub me rub me."

He let more weight come into play. Oh, luscious sounds. Lust-insanity to penetrate grew gigantic, yet the agony of withholding prevailed. The male ache increased.

His left hand came up from below and tangled in her hair. He guided her head into the position he wanted, flashing his eyes inside hers for a wounding second, and opened her mouth with his, launching a giant kiss, its eroticism uninhibited and voluptuous. Her tongue tantalized, taunting him to chase it around inside the kiss, sometimes in her mouth, sometimes in his. Never, not for an instant, did his cock cease its rub, perfectly positioned against the sensitive folds of the yoni.

When she reached the edge of screaming inside the kiss, he stood up taller, forcing her head to bend further in supplication. It brought the underside of his cock more rudely in contact with her bud, the sure path up they had followed hundreds of times. He poured his mouth into her above and let his weight tell below.

At the first strong clench of her pelvis, he pulled out of the kiss to watch her face, saw the sure sign of the going, the going before the coming, and soon the sailing afar of body and soul, her breath running away like a horse wild with fright, eyes widening from a shocking vision fast approaching, skin flushing red, and that distinctive scent, like an exotic mushroom steeped in musk.

Her uninhibited bellow shook the walls. "Oh oh oh oh. Oh no, no, no, no fucking no."

"All gone," he said, whispering into her screams. "All gone."

He continued to caress her organs with his cock all through her flight to its shuddering, gripping end, continuing to rub as she floated free, her mouth open emitting lovely descent-vowels. Then she drifted back to earth, looking unraveled – no attempt to hasten composure – deliberately letting him see her carnal satisfaction, hear her heavy breathing filled with little words of endearment, dirty ones and sweet ones.

"That was a good one," she said with a laugh, eventually, with shiny eyes, still nearly breathless, clinging to his body like a primate on a tree-trunk. "My toes curled good."

He rocked his pelvis, to keep alive the heat as yin pressed yang. She cooed with each motion, and then looked him straight in the eye.

"My turn now. Do what I say."

He nodded.

"Put it in," she said, voice aching and naked.

The tip lowered. The shaft changed angle. He let his weight fall, and the puffed lips parted sweetly. Like a forlorn sojourner finding the way, he slid in. Wet insides encased him. The sweet sadness vanished.

He thrust in, hard, many times. She could not speak, only give gurgling grunts on each stroke. He stopped to regroup. She whispered in his ear. "Push my legs apart."

He did it with urgent roughness, which made her cry out. He resumed thrusting.

"Yes, yes, split me, fuck me. Fuck. Me. Like. That. Like. That. Like. That."

"Yes.

"Open me, fuck me."

"Yes."

"Hard, fuck me, fuck me."

He stood stronger than ever, planted on the floor, moving inside her with power. The sounds and scent of sex surrounded them, bringing him right to the edge of his own going. At the first sign she laughed.

"There. There you go now."

He passed all striving, setting free his strategies, let them be taken up, swept away. Nothing could stop them from winning.

"Give me," she said. "Splash me."

Her hands gripped the vanity tabletop to brace for it. She removed her legs from his waist, held them away from his body with strong thigh muscles, more split-apart than ever. A sensation of entering a secret sanctuary sent his stomach falling, falling.

A final, massive stroke. His voice roared out.

In her vagina the spray deluged the flesh, soaking it thick and warm. He emptied all in, splash after splash.

They stayed joined and finished long, with laughter and looks, long looks of pleasure and the most intimate truths that can be. They did not avoid these reflecting in each other's eyes. She squeezed. He contracted his shooting muscles to feel his organ pulse inside the slippery warmth.

"This is what you do to a girl," she said.

"Yes."

"You love her, she wants sex."

"Yes."

"She'll beg for it."

Finally, she eased off the vanity to stand in his embrace, still filled with cock. She didn't want to let it go, she said, don't take it out, she said, don't ever take it out, she said.

He did, though.

Then, he watched to see if she would carry out the plan. She reached for the clean black cotton under-thing lying on the bed. With deliberate grace, she pulled the tiny garment over hips.

"All nice and cozy," she said, tugging it into place, fitted into the delta. "All nice in me."

She reached for her dress lying across a chair, an ephemeral blue, with spaghetti straps. A shudder ran through him when she settled the dress in place having donned nothing else under. Very few women could bring this off with taste and modesty yet still allow a simmering tease for the eyes. After a quick run of a brush through her hair, stockings that had their own way of staying up, and simple pumps, she was put together, a lovely package with a ripe liquid center.

He savored every detail of this femme dance while slipping into his dinner clothes.

This is how you want it, the echo of a female screaming with sexual joy in your ears, your own libido drained out, its juice soaking the womb of your lover.

She lifted her face to him, glowing with color and heat, the flush of orgasm her only makeup. He knew the primal scent was strong on her skin. So too, for him.

"As you requested, this is how I'll be. All evening. Aware of ... inside," she said.

"Every once in a while, look at me a certain way. Show me you're feeling it, right then. Specifically. Squeezing."

"Like this?"

Watching her expression, his chest filled with the thrill of her unashamed daring.

"Yes."

"Okay."

"Let's go. I hope you're hungry, this dinner's going to be very special."

"As long as there's chocolate at the end," she said.

above the canyon

Against the face of a steep-sided canyon below Mulholland, right at the back of its curving hollow, a house clung magnificently. Where once only chaparral and struggling dessert sage prevailed, a genius had deployed determined pull upon official Beverly Hills and caused the vertical to manifest something normally calculated in the horizontal and coveted ferociously in that town – real estate.

As if unsatisfied by his feat of property ex nihilo, the magician elevated the drama by erecting an audacious edifice. The design permitted no mitigation of the slope, no grading, no terracing. Instead, outsized steel girders impaled the cliff again and again. Supported by and growing from these, fixed at sundry and unpredictable elevations, crystalline shapes balanced, indented, hung, and cantilevered. At the bottom of the property – literally at the bottom – two mighty steel members, anchored in unapologetic industrial style, angled up into and abutted the crystal forms, as if holding the house up against the cliff like a giant warrior rudely hanging a picture.

As might be expected, no relief from the threat of gravity could be found inside. Many floors were transparent. A stair up from one room to another curved out into space nakedly. In several places, boulders denuded of sand and earth intruded into rooms, formed their very walls, glass sheets riveted into the primal rock. Massiveness everywhere foretold disaster. Yet always, just when sense predicted downfall, the anxious eye would discover a counterforce, strong enough, placed smartly.

Here one might exhaust oneself seeking assurances, which would never be found – except in surrender to the power of the builder.

~~~~~

"I like the cold on my nose," he said.

"Me too."

"It's hard to get cold like this in Los Angeles."

"Who'd you have to bribe?" she asked.

"Something even money can't buy."

"I'm glad you bought this comforter," she said, moving it across her torso. "So fine. Pounds of down. Well, at least a pound. And not just down, it's eider down."

"You read the tag?"

"Yeah. And the fabric, the cotton. Gorgeous. Silky."

One of the softest things ever to touch her body, she said. Could snuggle in for days, she insisted. Adored being wrapped in this cold night, she remarked, as did he, both otherwise naked, outside, up on the highest point of the place, a cantilevered landing at the end of two narrow walks that crossed between an observation deck above one wing of the house and the master bedroom topping the other. Up above everything.

Just after midnight.

"I love it on my breasts."

"I noticed."

"... sliding it on them. Like this."

"We like to watch when a girl touches herself."

"We?"

"Boys."

"Men?"

"Men."

"By the way, it's okay for boys to call us 'girls,' as long as you know we are women."

"Got it. Knew it. Meant it."

She continued her self-caress.

"You like touching yourself," he said.

She nodded slowly and meaningfully, holding his eyes. "But more when you touch them," she said. "Want to?"

"Keep wearing tops like that one you had on

tonight, I won't be able to keep my hands off."

"They looked nice in that shirt?" she asked.

"They were like fruits waiting for me to pick them."

"Which fruit?"

"Or at least get at them from under, find out if they are ripe."

"You're turning me on." She hissed in a breath. "Which fruit?"

"A mango."

"What?"

"No, don't get all pouty, a mango's the wrong shape. I just said that because they look as good as mangos taste." He looked off to the side, into the dark of the canyon below. "Like peaches taste, too, and cantaloupes and how about ... nectarines."

"Breasts like nectarines?"

"Breasts you can get nectar from."

It made her groan. "Please try that to get that. Please. Please," she whispered, softer with each word. Her arms rose above her head to leave the rest undefended, hair spread around like a halo on the pillows, body swaying as if humming a love song. The invitation was unmistakable.

He pulled the blanket a little, revealing the hollows under her arms.

"Please make them bare," she said.

She squirmed under the fabric, inching it imperceptibly down, arching her back as if to spill it off.

"Won't ripe fruit suffer in the cold?" he asked.

"Make them suffer a little. Then take the nectar in your mouth."

Mercy.

He slid the cover to make the tips emerge, puffy and begging.

"They *are* ripe," he said.

"Drink them. Kiss them and drink them."

He worshiped her breasts, then. So plump, the softest of soft flesh. A nipple swelled in his mouth. Lifting off, leaving it wet and exposed to the air, then recaptured with lips. She shifted her torso to help him attend to the other, whimpering pathetically, making the bright keening sounds that seem like pain yet are not. She did not lower her arms, a gesture of surrender.

"Kiss them," she hissed.

He liked the begging. She kept pleading to be kissed, tugged, and bitten. He exceeded her instructions. She tossed and wriggled under his mouth, which grew more outrageous in extremes.

His hand slid between her thighs. Certainly, nectar there. He spread slick girl juices onto the waiting tiny bud. Her back arched high, body taut. His fingers slipped inside. Open. Ready.

"Oh my God, oh please, oh please..."

He lifted his body over hers. Her thighs

parted to give him his place for sweet
penetration.

"Oh no oh no oh no."

"Yes," he grunted.

Electricity raced between touchpoints,
flashing as the eyes of one caught the
undefended abandon in those of the other. She
kept her arms above her head, even as they
ascended in a spectacular flight above the high
nest, above the canyon, above the cold Los
Angeles night.

The low-pressure system departed before
morning. A high swept in, and now provided
the opposite pole of Angeleno winter extremity
– eighty-one in January.

No amount of sun could fully chase every
pocket of chilly air out from the crevices of the
cliff-face, even with sea-gusts from the Pacific
Ocean swirling. A reservoir of cool lingered
under the cantilevered floors of the house as
well, and the massive rocks entrenched in the
walls formed a sink for the cold.

Nevertheless, on the ascension of the sun
into afternoon, someone opened every window
in the structure, including those looking
skyward. The house filled with breezes. No
matter where one turned, large pots and glass
bowls full of tulips and hyacinths shivered
when caught by one of these miracle zephyrs,
imparting scent to the warm winter wind inside

the house.

The unknown caretaker also switched on a waterfall fountain that began at the top cube and descended in a chain of gullies and pools through half the house's spaces to gather in a minimalist three-foot square pond, forty-two feet below origin. This pool served as the centerpiece for a generous inside-outside garden.

They were enjoying a picnic there.

"More wine, please."

Yes, the teasing in her voice, the first piece of erotic play today. They had been busy, out. Separate ways. Now the out-business-dragons lay dead in Santa Monica and Century City, and they were in.

"The wine's getting warm. Should've brought an ice bucket down here," he said as he poured.

"I like it when it warms up a little. Lets more oak-taste free."

"A lot of wine people in France mock the lust we Americans have for that oakey-smokey taste in our Chards, you know," he said.

"So? That just makes me want to put this one back in the barrel two more years. So there."

"Your usual contrarian reaction," he said.

"Damn arrogant Frenchy attitude. Someone's got to smirk at them like they do at us. Screw them. Bring on the oafish American wine!"

"I like your 'other-than' with everything," he said.

"You shouldn't tell me that. I might other-than you."

"My goal is to inflame your buzz-off attitude to the world all the better to exaggerate your simpatico with me," he said.

She looked at him with a soundless smile, holding his gaze over the rim of her wineglass.

"You liked that one, didn't you?"

She nodded.

"You like to tease with words," he said.

"Yes.

"Does it count as oral sex?"

"Yes. Say something else." She leaned forward for this game.

"When your words have sting in them, it's like the tip of your tongue when we're kissing. Drives me crazy."

"Oh."

"It happened the other day when I came to pick you up at the office. You were giving someone a hard time. Something about overtime."

"Yeah, I remember," she said. "It was the lead person for one of our minor clients. He tried to pull a fast one."

"I didn't catch everything, but the last thing I heard you say was, 'Only I can get away with shit like that, and I don't try'."

"Yes." She smiled at him.

"I got a virtual erection from that speech."

"You did?"

"Made me want to be really bad and try to get away with something."

They ate in silence for a few minutes. He fixated on a vegetable pâté obtained from a shop on Beverly. She had swiped at it once or twice before returning to her cold poached bass with lemons, thus the layered square of pastry and savory vegetables was his to ravage. He attacked it with a piece of baguette as a spoon.

He noticed her movements slowing. He knew that to be a sign of her libido stirring, a trait he had learned of her in their ten days' time. She centered on him with intent.

"If it stays this warm this evening, does that mean the comforter will be too much?"

"No," he said.

"It won't get over-hot? Overheated?"

"That's the beauty of it. In warm weather, it breathes enough to let you be comfortable, and it's so light –"

"Because I can't get it out of my mind."

"– it doesn't feel like a hot blanket on you."

"So soft," she whispered, her smile expanding. It thrilled, being the choice of a woman who turned herself on this well. This often. This fast. Such a thing requires courage for a man, since he controls her not – yet so much more the implications of being freely chosen by a strong femme.

"You deserve everything soft," he said.

"That's our theme? Soft?"

"You'd allow it?"

"I could be voracious in it," she said. "Relentless. Ridiculous. About everything soft. Consider yourself warned."

"I hope to rise to the challenge."

She shook her head slowly at the awful pun, but did not cool. She took more wine and a last bite of her dinner.

"What do I do that you like? That's soft?" he asked, challenging.

"The inside of your mouth is really soft," she said. "I like putting my tongue in there."

"Hmmm."

"Slow, just a little in. To find yours."

"I love this," he said. "We're sitting here, a civilized dinner, good wine, adult and sophisticated, but talking about sex like teens all hot after necking for two hours."

"Am I going too fast?" she asked.

"No."

"Do we talk too much?"

"No."

"Men usually don't want to talk about sex. To a woman."

"No?"

"About anything."

"I'm not that guy. Go."

"Who's better at the talking, me or you?

We're both showing off."

"You."

"Did you ever kiss a girl for at least two hours and talk about sex with her in-between kisses?"

"No."

"Oh, that's too bad."

"Wait … yes, once. Wow, I haven't thought about her in a while."

"Her name?"

"Shara Ann Marland."

"She was a talker?"

"Yes. We agreed to not have sex, she was fifteen, but she let me kiss her as much as I wanted, then she used words on me. Talking about the ways of kissing and touching, saying the names of body parts. Maybe Shara was the one who started me being a talker about sex. Made me like talking about it. Yeah, I'd say she was the one who showed me you could turn the ordinary into something erotic and gigantic. By talk."

"I like this Shara," she said. "Then after talking about your mouth and her mouth and the juices in them and everything, you started kissing again?"

"Yeah. For another hour. Our faces were raw. She had that wild look in her eyes, like you had last night."

"I don't think you understand," she said. "Last night blew a few circuits."

"It did?"

"You lit me up twice."

"Yeah."

"The fire's not out. I've been obsessing ever since, especially, you know, about the down blanket on my breasts. More or less constantly. Didn't stop all day. I was in a meeting with three people, talking fast, dishing right and left, and the sound of your voice saying 'nectarines' kept going off in my little brain."

"Sheesh."

"After an hour, I had to go into the women's room, shut the door behind me ... and tend to my forest fires."

"Oh my God."

"I opened the first few buttons of this blouse, it's Ann Taylor, so I could look down and see the tips being –"

"I like this Ann Taylor."

"– to see the nipples pushing. When I closed my eyes, I could imagine the softness of that damned down comforter and the shape of your mouth on me. Your mouth on me... last night ... for so long. I kept my hands between my legs and rubbed myself all the way gone."

"Really."

"Really. I had to be careful, no screaming. It was a quiet one. You know I like to scream."

"Yes."

"Now, it's your turn. What part of me is softest?" she asked.

"In your mind's eye, where you were rubbing this afternoon?"

"Yes?"

"Hold the lips open in your imagination and let me touch inside. That's my choice. Just inside. Where it's soft."

"Somehow I knew that would be your choice. Every girl believes she's really soft there. But there are only a few boys who care. Mostly, boys don't go slow enough to care about it."

"There's another thing girls do that's soft."

"What?"

"Another thing women do, I mean. Girls don't know how to do this."

"What?"

"Wrap themselves in something beautiful, something precious and delicate," he said, "so they can be unwrapped by their lover for sex. For instance, like this."

He presented a box he had kept hidden. It was elegant, enfolded in high-gloss platinum-colored paper held closed by a black wax seal.

"What is it?" She cleaned her hands on a wet-nap and dipped them in the pool, then dried off.

"Something soft."

She glanced over at him once as she worked open the seal and unfolded the paper and box it covered. With delight, she lifted a shimmering gossamer thing, a garment of silk.

"Oh, oh. Oh dear," she whispered.

The color was remarkable, pale cream, importantly influenced by the blue-green elements of aquamarine. She gave off little sighs and exclamations as she held it by fingertips and turned it in the low angles of the waning winter sun.

"The color," she said. "Did you do that on purpose?"

He nodded. "You let me look so long in your eyes last night, this color saturated me. Infected me. I got more lost in that green, the deeper you let me see in. When I saw this thing in the store today, I could barely breathe."

That deserved a smoky look, he believed. She did not disappoint. She collapsed the silk garment into her lap and leaned forward.

"Outrageous," she said. "Don't stop talking. More. More."

"That's all I could think about the whole time I was buying it."

"The color of my eyes?"

"Yes."

"They infected you?"

"I fell into them."

"That's advanced. It's tenth date."

"See, I'm moving fast."

"You already got sex from me. Fast."

"I want to go even faster," he said.

"You already have sex. You already have me talking. You already have me letting you look in my eyes. But eye contact during sex is tenth date, if ever, and we've only had a few. So, no."

"Speed up with me."

"Where are you going?"

He paused to let her know they had paused.

"To be in love."

"I don't want to fall in love."

"Yes, you do."

"No."

"It won't slow down the sex."

"Yes, it will," she said.

"The chance to fall in love with you is fueling my sex drive."

"Oh, for crying out loud."

"Actually ... it's the chance you'll fall in love with me."

She did not run for the door. She did not get annoyed. She did not look away from him. She cocked her head with chin raised.

"Prove it," she said.

"Prove what?"

"Prove I want to fall in love."

He only had to pause about twenty seconds.

"Okay, close your eyes."

She froze.

"Only to help you visualize, that's all."

When she did it, he moved closer. Their knees pressed. "Let our sex buildup go in neutral. Don't worry about it. We'll rev it up again in a minute. Keep your eyes closed and tell the truth."

She took a deep breath, then nodded.

"You're not sleeping with anyone else the past ten days," he said.

"No."

"Or flirting. Or looking."

"No."

"Even though I didn't ask."

"Right."

"You don't fantasize about another man when we're all hot."

"No."

"When I'm inside you."

"No."

"Or kissing."

"No."

"Imagine we haven't had sex yet. Just this verbal teasing and laughing together. A few dates in L.A. Great wine and food. But no sex.

"Really?"

"Yes. Fun yes, sex no. We're playing hard to get."

"Hmmm..."

"You would still want to be with me, to tangle with me. There's something there. Besides sex. You're interested."

She opened her eyes. "No. All I want from you is sex."

He let that shoot right past. She had wavered saying it, he was certain, by a flicker at the corner of her mouth. He held steady, silent, letting her declaration begin to ring hollow. It already had barely enough life to bounce off the wall, and it grew more frail with each second. She began to break down in two directions, a giddy giggle and heavy breathing.

He did not move a muscle.

She stood up and walked around the garden, the limpid silk shirt grasped in her left hand. Bluster, laughter, and agony followed one another in her voice. Once or twice, she glanced over at him. Laughing began to win. From ten feet away, she took aim.

"You bastard," she said.

He rose and walked to her side.

"You are interested."

She paused to let that hang in the air. Then she sighed and spoke.

"I'll admit one thing, and then you'll let go."

"Okay."

"I'll probably regret this."

"Say it."

"I feel this drop of girl-happiness to be with you – for other than sex. It's tiny. Nothing to get married over. Tiny. Sweet and cute. Tiny."

He put his arm around her waist and pressed his hip against hers. Her face was soft. In all the bluster, she had not shed a tear.

"You've got quite a grip on that shirt," he said.

"I'm never letting go of it."

"We were saying how I tried to match it with the color of your eyes."

"It's exactly right, I think."

"I know."

"It's very beautiful," she said, her libidinous energy returning. She held the garment with one hand by the thin straps, running the other hand down its length. "Soft indeed."

"That's right."

She brought some folds of the garment against her cheek and moved it against her skin. "Tell me how close you came."

He moved in. The lowering sun filled her eyes, lit them. He glanced at the fabric entwined around her fingers to consider the color of it, then back in her eyes.

"Very close."

"Yes?"

"But there are hundreds more colors in your eyes."

"Yes?" She kept moving the silk across her face.

"Maybe a thousand."

"It's beautiful. I love it." His heart thumped at her next move. Her hands went to the top of the blouse and began unbuttoning.

"I believe you. About thinking of my eyes when you were buying this gorgeous thing. Completely. But isn't it possible ..." she paused to get the third button undone, "... isn't it possible that there was something else, too?"

"What?"

"Well ... I would think ... based on what last night was like ..." she reached the final button,

"... what we were obsessed with, I would think you might also be thinking about ... my shape." She parted the blouse. There was a flesh-colored bra under. Her eyes disengaged from his, a signal he might wish to look down. As she moved sinuously in place, she continued verbal teasing.

"You know, this silk shirt you bought will be very tight."

"Yes."

"The silk is fine. But it's cut through with a certain amount of stretchy threads. It's not designed to be loose and flowy."

"Right."

She arched her back and let her hands fall to her sides. The blouse slumped off her shoulders, behind. It remained secure at the wrists.

"A woman buys a garment like this a size or two small, and pulls it on, even if it seems like it's the wrong size."

"That's what they told me."

"So, it's designed for one thing."

"Yes."

"To show off breasts."

"Yes."

"What I'm wearing now, underneath? That was supposed to do the same thing." She stood straighter and turned this way and that.

"Well, it does, and it doesn't," he said.

"What do you mean?"

"It shapes you, and that looks good. But ... you look so good bare ..."

"You prefer me bare?"

He nodded.

"With nothing holding anything up or covering?"

"Yes."

"You must have known, or did the salespeople tell you, you can't have a bra under a top like this. It would show every strap."

"Nobody told me."

"I believe you. You figured it out all by yourself, in your hot little imagination."

"Yes."

She laughed lightly. "So, in any event, I have to wear a camisole under, or be naked when I put it on."

"Apparently."

"How nice." She undid the cuffs of the Ann Taylor blouse and finished removing it from her body. The hands stayed in motion, went behind. She arched toward him, undid the clasps at the back, and dropped the bra away. She stood exposed in her confidence. He felt his obsession flame up and go roaring off.

"I'm putting this shirt on," she said.

"Hurry."

She positioned the opening of the garment over her head and worked her way into it, rolling it down over her torso, tugging the stretched fabric to set it in place. It fit close, like a taut second skin. The sleeves snugged down her arms to the wrists with hardly a wrinkle. The collar came far up her neck and embraced it.

Much to his delight, the bodice did not compress or misshape. The nipples made dents, as if protesting jail. He wanted them more than ever.

"Gorgeous."

"What a beautiful thing," she said. "I've got to look."

He followed her up one level of the house to a guest bedroom. She stood admiring in front of a mirror in its bathroom. She flounced her hair and shifted the garment with little tugs.

"Could they be any happier?" she cried, giggling, with a hand to her mouth. Indeed, there was no escaping the theme of this outfit – it was only about her curvy torso and the sweet nips at the top of the tips.

"It must feel good on your skin."

"Yes."

Then, no more teasing. He moved behind and circled his hands around, fitting them under and over, caressing. They watched this together in the mirror ... their faces ... his hands ... the sumptuous aqua-green hue and shimmer of silk.

"Your hands on me ..."

"Turn around," he ordered. She spun to face him.

"Lift it up. Not off." She positioned fingers at the hem of the shirt and peeled it up her body, gathering the folds in her hands and lifting until her breasts were exposed, offered, naked.

He took the nipples in his mouth, under his tongue and deeper in. His kisses moved from one to the other, causing groans in her throat.

"Bite them," she said.

Rougher. He pressed his tongue against the top of his mouth with the tip between and pulled, tugged, nipped. She yelped. They wiggled and swayed against each other.

She pulled the silk curtain down and spun away.

"I want to see the sunset while you kiss them," she said and ran out of the room.

He chased her up two levels. She waited out on the balcony of the living room, a perch above the canyon winding down to Los Angeles. She stopped him with a gesture as he approached. Her hands worked their way under the shirt. They caressed.

"Do you like when I touch them?" she asked. He nodded. "How did you say it last night?"

"Boys like watching girls touch themselves."

"I like you watching."

"Do it for an hour."

"You don't think it's odd if I obsess about them, like you? Weird?"

"Are you kidding?"

"A girl has to love her own body, you know."

"That's right," he said.

"They're just breasts, no big deal, but both of us seem to think they're holy and sacred, or something."

He laughed. "They are eternal."

"I like to touch myself. But it's not enough." She took the hem in her fingertips again. She lifted the shirt.

"I still need you devouring them."

He ran to her and took the raspberries in his mouth again.

"Kiss them kiss them kiss them," she begged. Sacredly.

They kissed and caressed there on the open terrace as the sun went to the rim of the Pacific. They removed each other's garments. The air floating up the canyon drifted around her nearly nude body, expanding her scent. He inhaled it with eyes closed while her kisses rained over his chest and shoulders. Eventually, the silk shirt was the only garment still on either of them.

"Not here," she said suddenly, pulling away.

"No?"

"Telescopes." She laughed and ran past him.

Declining three rooms in the center of this level, she circled all the way to the opposite side, the east side. To his bedroom.

He approached. She was not smiling now. She tried to remove the silk shirt. He stopped her with a raised hand and a look.

"Leave it on."

She nodded.

"It can be washed. I asked."

She understood.

The incredible down comforter covered the bed. He yanked it off onto the floor. She climbed onto the sheets fast. Her thighs flew open. He brought his body over. The cock hovered. She was so ready, slick inside, set free by their teasing talk, his thrust went home like iron slipping into velvet.

"Oh ohhh." An agony-shock of penetration.

They positioned to give her a rub, sex on sex. Her left hand went there. Smart left hand.

"My forests are burning."

He waited until her fingers began caressing around the buried shaft. His rhythm began, the march of a victor, the thrusting so rich and pure it immediately destroyed her sanity.

"Oh woh moe foe, oh fuck fuck fuck."

He aimed for the roof of vagina. She grunted on each stroke, with squealing rage the better he hit the target. Then, a chant from her lust-heart.

"Fuck me. Fuck me. Right there. Oh fuck. Right. There. Right. There."

Wildness in her eyes, those subtle-green eyes, open points of loving flashing to take stroke after stroke. Her liquids flowed. Carnal scent filled the bed.

He turned her over and dominated from behind. She groveled into the sheets and screamed into a pillow. He stroked her a hundred times like that, with more punishment than any of their times before.

With a yell of protest, she slipped him out and spun onto her back.

"Like this," she said, lifting her legs high up and apart. He penetrated at once.

"Oh yes oh yes oh yes oh yes oh yes."

It could never be a mistake, what he believed of her, what she was lying about, what would come true if he gave her a thousand orgasms and brought his sheltering strength into bed, draping it around them, a cover for the cold dawn.

She thrashed on the bed but did not block each stroke plunging dead center, shifting hips and pelvis for the shaft to go true, the unprotectedness making him roar. He slammed in on sheer power, thudding to the bottom of her sex, heavy, grunting, ramming strokes, which took roughness and transformed it to triumph for both of them. She went wildly unglued, screaming a word on each penetration.

"Oh. No. No. No. Oh. Fuck. Oh. Fuck. Oh. Fuck."

A certain rich stroke went home. An

endgame tightness under the rim of his cock turned him inward. He left her to her fate.

Now each thrust charged through his body – a man filling with fire, destined to erupt, the wet ripping sounds of the thrusts urging it, and the whimpering in her voice.

Five, six, seven more massive strokes all the way in. On the last, his rage began to spill. A heavy splash flooded the cervix. A second – his cock slipped from between her legs and aimed at her torso, where silk-covered breasts taunted him, incited him, thrilled him with their begging nipples and perfect roundness.

On the third gorgeous spurt, her hands held the shirt high up and away from her breasts. While most it spurted across them and their tips, hot juice splashed on her fingers holding the precious silk. He contracted mightily, growling and swearing, until empty.

She smiled up at him, flushed and trembling from orgasm, her body laced with warm white liquid ribbons, the shirt anointed with them.

"Yes. Yes, oh yes," she said, delirious. "Now I have your nectar."

~~~~~

He tarried in a luscious dream.

Weightless in the fragrant liquid world of it, time flowed with a beautiful languor, attending the beat of his quiescent heart.

Then, the waking whisper. He ascended, seeking a white porcelain bowl filled with berries, desiring their essence on his lips.

He blinked away the night-dream, the better to grasp the reality an arm's length away. She was awake. She did not avoid him seeing her watching.

His sight sharpened. He spoke.

"Really. You only want sex?"

She rotated in the bed to put her back to him, to put her visage away. Too late – as her face disappeared, he caught the glimmer of melted honey in her aquamarine eyes.

where only joy was

A siren wailed away in the distance, fading. It woke her. In her usual way, she gauged the time by her sleep cycles and the sound level outside. It was 3:30-ish, she was certain.

Happiness appeared, clear and clean in a deep pool. It rose from laughter, from sexual gratification, from sure knowledge he was faithful. Her hips moved in it like those of a serene swimmer, languorous in slow liquids. Even as she arrived fully awake, the happiness did not recede.

She stood up from the bed amid local chaos – a deformed candle on the floor, some feathers flung, furniture pushed around. She smiled at a heavy armchair on its side in the corner. Its sight returned her to the moment, just a few hours ago, when she clung to it desperately, sobbing with joy, legs parted, his mouth buried between.

She looked down at him sleeping on his left side. Her attention followed his breath once, twice, again. She moved around the bed and sat on the edge, gently, then lay her hand on his hip.

When no reaction followed, she set her hand at the jut of the hipbone and pulled firmly until he rolled onto his back. Amazingly, he settled without waking.

The fine cock lay exposed. The moon shone upon it. With no rush, no agenda, she let time drift, enjoying the sight unalloyed, having no less liking for it soft and plump than engorged and amok. Several times she was self-aware of outright pleasure in gazing at it with entire attention, as long as she wished.

Eventually, her fascination became a subtle call centered in her pelvis, a faint throb. Even content as she was, the stirring of appetite delighted, as if announcing more life were always to be offered.

Appraising her mood and all qualities of the night, she took him in her hand with confidence, clasping the soft folds of skin over the shaft, slipping down to the base to locate the core of a new erection. He stirred. His eyes opened. He shifted to be perfectly flat on the bed. They exchanged one clear glance before she lowered her lips to the tip, let her tongue form a cushion under, and with delicacy, eased her mouth well down the length, the tip approaching the opening of her throat, nestling in place, not deep enough to gag. She tilted, rotated, and elongated, opening wider the harder he became. Movement stopped – she held him deep and still.

"Fuck ..." he said, within a long sigh.

When she gave no sign of letting him out, he matched her by offering no sign of thrusting. His breathing reflected arousal from being sucked all the way down, but soon began to slow. The only convulsion – a series of strong contractions of his buttocks, a man's way of putting the hardest, longest finish on his erection. Her mouth and throat accommodated, discovering the right position to enable breathing around, to keep from tensing up, and so to achieve a peaceful but salacious state of yin/yang – him engulfed, her penetrated.

"I need a second," he whispered.

This was a prearranged signal, which she suspected might fly. With grace, she drew off, leaving her mouth's wetness glimmering on the shaft in the moonlight.

So beautiful it bruises my heart, the outrageous cock of him, tender and dangerous.

She turned her face to his. Oh, she liked it very much, quite so, that he could not look her in the eye just then, mesmerized by her mouth as he was. She let him gaze at it for long seconds, licking her lips once or twice.

She slipped off the bed and led him by the hand into the bathroom. Sliding open the glass door of the shower, she turned on a light pressure of water, angling it sharply to hit the tiled wall. She fitted herself against his side, and cradled her hand under his penis, hard, jutting and impatient. With an animal sound of gratification, he released a steady stream, strong on an upward arch against the wall and cascading water. There had been a quantity of wine that evening, so they were there a time.

After washing, they padded back to the bed, again with his hand in hers. He tumbled in, and with no 'by your leave,' and none needed, assumed his former place. With one last glimpse into his eyes, she folded her body into a comfortable position, put her lips right on the tip, and with even more gentleness and certainty than before, slid his cock completely inside, down to the root, the head again finding home at the opening of her throat. Amid a few of his groans and swear words, and a few more of the sharp jerks of his organ, they found a way to stay in place, joined.

She held for several moments in readiness for him to thrust, or for something to be not quite right. In keeping with the perfection of this magical night, his breathing evened and eventually slowed. *How lordly, to have her mouth at his service and not do anything about it.*

The night-quiet deepened. She made an adjustment to stay comfortable. With a deep sigh, she knew this carnal kiss must end.

But then, an image. She saw herself once removed, bringing sharp awareness of the plain reality of herself folded on the bed, body offered, cock filling her mouth, while the swirl of humanity filled the planet and the earth spun under the silent sun.

Sacred or profane? She sent her consciousness inside her lips, sliding down on him a fraction to feel the reality of thick flesh forcing her mouth open. She tilted her head to feel it, his organ, buried in her, her tongue pillowing the underside of it.

With the depth of their love and trust, this magnificent thing would chase her and fuck her thousands of times. Oh, she loved it.

Then, even though she remained motionless, she imagined her mouth opening even more, felt the sexiness of it, widening with no limit, exposed to him infinitely. She imagined releasing her weight, easing herself down, far down, his organ sliding completely into her throat and beyond, its tip finally touching a spot deep between her breasts. In this way, she took him into her heart, where only joy was.

When her worship of them ended and she slipped off, he was truly asleep. She covered and cradled his body. The pool of happiness in which she swam flowed gold and rich now. She put her face to his skin to inhale his scent in her dreams.

wanting her scent close

Silk.
Everything in the top three drawers.
His hands touched garments – light, soft, each as ethereal as a spun-sugar cloud, every item flawlessly clean, folded with care, and lovingly arranged. The panoply of shimmering hues added to his pleasure. He saw not one harsh color, but many striking shades, for silk takes pigment with a signature subtlety. Had he not removed each one from her body at one time or another? His hand and eye were not jaded in rediscovery of beauty in these things.

"I have my hand in your drawers."

She took his pun with a slight smile. "Don't get anything wet," she said. He was naked and amorous, so it was a legitimate caution.

"Does boy-stain come out of silk?"

"Does girl?"

"By the perfection of everything here, and the amount of sex we've put them through, we must have proven both by now."

"Oh yes."

"So, no inhibitions on that count."

"No." She walked over to him to deliver the next words with emphasis, diverting his attention from the garments by the closeness of her naked body.

"Let's test, anyway," she said.

"Deliberately?"

She nodded.

"Excessively?"

She nodded.

They held eyes steadily, registering understanding and agreement. Surely this was the essence of their eroticism, such looks silently making carnal purpose clear.

"Then I want the very best thing you have," he said.

"Open the bottom drawer."

He savored the beautiful dark wood and heavy build of the lingerie cabinet – it had to be intentional, that jolt from the contrast of a few dozen ounces of clothing secured and safe because of one hundred pounds of thick walnut. The yin-yang of that incited the mood.

He found an elegant box in the bottom drawer. It must have been recently purchased – he had never seen it. Naturally, it was over-heavy. The boards of the box were covered with linen, an off-white shade. It opened like the folio of a fine manuscript, untying with satin ribbons that held it closed by being wound around porcelain buttons.

From inside, from within layers of tissue, he extracted an exquisite thing, a camisole, crafted of the softest, the lightest, the quintessence of silk. What color? No, not white. No. Somewhere in it, furtive in the folds, shimmering in the liquid flow as he held it by straps to let it unfurl, both blue and green might be seen – yet that was as if braying the name of two colors. No, the faintest whisper of aqua only. Not even that of the sea, for that would be too harsh as well. So weightless was this garment, so fragile, it must have been breathed into life by the will of a goddess, and only by the least of her whispers, and that must have been the moment the tinge of color fell upon it.

"That's an impossible garment," he said in awe.

"Yes."

"It cost hundreds, didn't it?"

She nodded, admiring it with him.

His hand stroked it once, the caress conveying the exciting illusion of having felt nothing. He noticed his sensitivity reset accordingly – the garment shifted the gage of touch in seduction.

"It's almost like you have to be quiet when you put it on."

"Yes. And clean. And smooth."

She took steps away from him to stand before the full-length mirror in the corner of her dressing area. He believed she might have been

born expressly that this thing might have a
woman suitable for it. As subtle as, being small in
all proportion, with curves that implied, did not
exaggerate. As light as, having that way of
weightlessness when standing or moving. As
smooth as, he saw again as she turned to appraise
herself in the mirror, for there was nothing
inelegant anywhere, no blemish or rough skin.

"You even have the right haircut," he said.
Short, shaped, simple. Revealing.

She floated back toward him. He gathered the
camisole into his hands and held it out. Her arms
went in first, then her head. He flowed the
garment down her torso, letting it settle in place.
It terminated provocatively at the bottom of her
slightly rounded belly, above the bare mons. It
was tailored well, for it clung and hung at the
same time, revealed and cloaked, even though
nearly transparent. The neckline and subtly
gathered bodice made a glorious definition of her
breasts, an unapologetic worship of them.

"I pity the poor man who only thinks it's sexy
to take things off a woman," he said.

"That's true. But what about the pants? That
could be more difficult," she said, looking down
at her bare areas below the hem of the camisole.
"How will you stand covering me there?"

He lifted the other half of the ensemble from
the box. Same silk, same ephemera, same mere
suggestion of color. The pants slithered in his
hand. As if by magical conjoining of their libidos,

she raised her right leg and set its foot on the edge of a dressing table at the same time his hand fit between her legs and shaped to her sex – it was all one gesture. She rested her left hand on his shoulder to balance and looked in his eyes to expose her pleasure.

He touched with devotion. How thrilling to caress the lips through the silk. How sensual the perception of fabric melting as it took up her wetness. How wonderful she was naked of hair – nothing but bare skin and slick juice.

"Open me."

He slipped two silk-covered fingers partially inside, spreading gently to ease her apart. More of the garment became wet through this.

"I adore being opened by your hands," she whispered. "I love it. Open me."

"You can't imagine how soft it feels," he said, caressing the lips and glans.

"Let me see." She brought her free right hand to tangle in the fabric, and taking one side of the lips, pulled the opening wider. Their hands met and began to move together, with true lovers' understanding.

Her breathing increased depth and speed, the ascent of arousal precious to him. He helped her along by urging his phallus against her hip.

Her fingers were inside now.

"It's so creamy," she said. "Doesn't it make you want to thrust right in it?"

"Slam in. We shouldn't take away all the

wetness."

"So I can be properly fucked?" she asked. Perhaps no one on earth had ever said it so melodiously. She was so gentle, the edges of the rude word tore at their mutual sensibility, but failed to rip it apart, another provocative yin/yang.

"Yes."

They inspected the pants. They were damp in many places, darker patches on the fine silk surface. He raised the thing to his face, wanting her scent close, knowing such a gesture would inflame.

"Let me, too."

He brought the fabric to her cheek and mouth and trailed it over her neck. Inhaling. Flashing arousal in her eyes. A deep sigh.

She took the garment, lowered her leg, bent over, put one foot after the other in the openings and pulled it up and over hips. In his belly, a tug of regret when her bare sex disappeared.

She walked in a graceful circle to show the outfit. He desired her body all the more for it being covered. Jealous of the silk.

"Angelic," he said.

"Do you forgive me for saying that word?" she asked. "The F-word?"

"This is the Garden of Eden. There's no sin here."

She took him by the hand and led him to the side of the bed. He fell back on it, cock erect, jutting strongly.

She climbed on the bed to straddle him, pulled the fabric of the pants aside to expose the pouty lips, and lowered her hips. The kiss of labia on the head, then liquid engulfing as she descended – like being swallowed by a satin cloud.

"Me," she said. "Let me."

"Oh, yes, go, yes."

Her hips began gliding. She didn't bounce, knowing he disliked it. He settled his hands on her waist to feel her body move. The touch seemed as if skin on skin, so ephemeral was the fabric of the camisole.

"Find your pleasure. Take it. I'll just be big and hard."

She engaged her dance, stroking down on him with the sheath of her sex, wiggling her pubic bone against his, then raising with the cock nearly free – to ready a new penetration. She made many such impalings. Sometimes she lifted off completely, pressed the lips against the underside of the erection, and rubbed well, forcing her clit against it. This was always followed by the plunge. A woman – adept, smart, limber.

She sparked off the impetus to go higher. That was exciting, she in charge, making their sex happen. He began to do what she did, often, when the going got going.

Poetry.

"Yes, like that, stroke me, stroke me, liquid girl – spill your honey on me."

She shifted legs and leaned forward to deliberately press her breasts against him through the silk camisole. That caused kissing. She dominated, with tongue withheld, until the heat overwhelmed, and she slid it between his lips. He took these kisses, deep as she wanted. She wiggled her torso against him while kissing, yet stayed in control of the hard thing below. After a pleasurable long time, she straightened, and her high ride resumed. The sight of her mouth as she rose nearly made him spurt off. They looked in each other's eyes to catch sparks of lust.

"Both mouths wet," he said.

"Yes."

"Yoni wet. Mouth wet."

"Yes."

"Yoni is smartest."

"Yes."

"Devour me with it."

That incited her rage. She had the position, the angle, and now unleased utter abandon in hips.

"It's so hard I can't melt it," she said.

"Drown it," he said.

He treasured the eclipse of her usual gentility, even beautiful and precious as it was to him and full of goodness – yes, he loved her that way. The sweet and gentle would return – but this carnal rush to ecstasy was immortal. His poetry increased to meet it.

"Sail away, sleek one in silk. Rub yourself on me. Sail away. You move like the girl of my dreams. I love it. Sail away."

She heeded these urgings, let them incite, offered her unguarded face to show joy in it. Hips, legs, and pelvis conspired to break her wide open on him, rutting, screaming, creaming, crying, rocking – and then screaming, screaming, vaulting over, reaching long, drawing it out, loosing every muscle, allowing all wetness rushing down between thighs with each convulsion. Her organs rippled around the thick thing that provoked her so, the shuddering in her breath wracking her body.

His hands on her sides felt everything.

She was beautiful.

Spasms ran through her muscles. Sex perfume hovered over the bed. He called her beautiful carnal names. After several minutes lying on top with her eyes turned away, coasting on saturation, she lifted her face to his.

"Your cock is so hard," she whispered, shaking her head in awe.

"You love rubbing it and fucking it."

"Yes."

"It is yours forever, for sex."

"Oh my God."

"Hard cock, always, to drop the tender yoni on when it's all soaking wet, when you're crazy with lust. For you to explode with the stars, all the time."

"It. Is. So. Fucking. Hard."

"Always there, for you to split yourself wide open on."

"I can't believe how much I want it. Cock."

"That's the best you ever used it. Our sex is getting better."

She nodded.

"The silk is all wet. The pants, anyway," he said.

"I liked it with them on, pulled to the side. The silk makes my body so sensitive. It's like another skin."

He tipped her over. His hand went between her legs. His cock came out as she rolled, and he put fingers in, instead.

Oh God, wet and creamy and smooth and silky inside the beautiful one.

He pushed her legs far apart on the bed and positioned between, right at his best angle, with the tip between open ripe lips. The sight of the aqua-white silk pulled to the side roused him. He thrust all the way in, quick, smooth, with a grunt.

"Oh, yes. Oh yes." She moaned with happy sorrow.

He looked in her eyes.

"Now to put boy stain on it," he said.

its wildest beast

This was a place much visited by ice. Repeatedly, over the past two million years, great sheets of it lumbered across the wide plain, unimaginably heavy, driven by the sullen power of the cold, the utterly cold North. In many places the ice measured two miles deep.

Every one-hundred thousand years the ice would recede, leaving boulders strewn at the terminus like a child abandoning cracked marbles on the pavement when called home.

Then, always the inexorable return, perhaps at a slightly different angle, perhaps slower or with a jerky movement, but always as destructive as previously, always from the North. Thus, another one-hundred thousand years of ice. Two miles deep.

A retreat in this colossal drama had played out just twelve-thousand years ago.

Now, in a moment between the times of ice, the land lived fast, running through seasons and decades, exploding in verdant grass each spring, suffering a blanket of snow when the sun hid beyond the horizon. The immense, lonely expanse remained untracked. Few herds of beasts crossed it. For many of the vast miles within its boundary, no human had walked there, ever.

~~~~~

Around noon, the phones went out of control. He heard his assistant call another agent into service. Funny, he rode above the tumult. Funny, because he had caused the commotion, but now watched the consequences unfold, detached.

It was a new discovery, found by him, a good seventy miles northeast of their 'profit boundary,' the line outside of which no pool of oil would be expected to pour forth a yield strong enough to justify extraction. Yet there it was, he saw on a map against the east wall of the office, that big blue pin stuck almost at the edge of the map like a drunken sailor's dart, somewhere it ought not be. The team sent out to perform a serious confirmation of his find had reported back this morning, in the affirmative.

"Alan, perhaps you need to call more people in," he said to his assistant.

"We'll be all right. There was a leak down in marketing, and it's just that too many people who shouldn't call, are calling here direct. Basically, they can't believe it. It'll die down in a little while, at least until the news is posted on our site."

The phone next to him rang again. Alan grabbed it and began speaking, fast.

He turned and headed back into his office. With the door closed, he left the hubbub behind. For a good while he just smiled, standing there in respectful appreciation of the rewards for being right.

A distinctive click signaled from the corner of the office. He walked across and peered at the device that had given it. A text message appeared on the small screen. The sender had elected not to piggyback images or voice, just a brief cryptic sequence of numbers.

"Print," he said. The device spit out a copy on paper immediately. Then, "Confirm."

Fifteen minutes found him walking up to his aircraft with leather tote in hand. He spoke with his mechanic. In the cockpit, he flipped on an instrument and keyed in the string of numbers. The dashboard displayed a heading and distance – an easy 212 miles, nearly due north. He wheeled out onto the tarmac and moments later shot into the sky.

~~~~~

Twelve thousand years ago, the last retreat of the ice deposited a gigantic pile of rubble and sand in a heaped-up ridge northwest of what later became Yellowknife, Northwest Territories, Canada. While weathered in the geological blink of an eye since, the rocky ridge remained a dramatic primitive feature on the post-glacial plain.

At the base of the most impressive section of the ridge stood a brilliant white structure. For eighty miles in any direction, not a soul, not a building, nothing in that entire expanse could be found. Nothing but grass. Directly adjacent this mysterious thing, two elegant airplanes sat parked, wingtip to wingtip.

The structure, a small pavilion, consisted of a fine but strong white fabric stretched by and strung over a skeletal assemblage of rods and posts, with members angling this way and that, all to establish an unusually shaped space sixteen feet across and high enough in which to stand. The cloth's thinness allowed a diffuse light to fill the chamber formed under the canopy. In many places, the white gave way to a fine screening material, which made some of the walls transparent, and allowed air to flow. There was a beautiful floor to the pavilion as well, consisting of a grid of structural members that could rest on earth or grass, on top of which fitted a checkerboard array of hardwood squares that linked up to form a sturdy platform eight inches above the ground.

Inside, on a luxurious arrangement of mats, pillows, and bedding, lay a couple stretched out side-by-side on their backs. They were naked. Against the amazing blue sky, the sea of verdant grass, and the expanse of white billowing around them like the sail of some fantastic sailing vessel, the skin of the lovers seemed a miraculous hue, deep black, lustrous black, like wet coal – amplified with a light sheen from recent exertion. That of the man, especially, seemed to invite touch, its hue and texture so striking it seemed one must set a hand there to investigate reality, even when it might have been known by looking.

His partner had been doing both. Even now her hip and thigh moved languorously against his side.

They had been talking of many things important after sex. They spoke of the thrill of flying across the leagues of grass to arrive at this spot in the trackless wild. She had much to say of her work in Toronto, difficult work, exacting, but rewarding to her purposefulness, and highly profitable. In turn she listened, fascinated, by the tale of his success in the last week here in the North. He checked to make sure nothing had altered her plan – she assured she would stay for the weekend before returning to the East.

At least they had the airplanes. Both accomplished pilots, they often met in places like this, since their perfectly matched craft could land in a short field, anywhere it was flat for 500 yards. For the next few days they would wander like luxurious nomads, floating above the earth, alighting in places of tranquility, perhaps featuring a watercourse with lonely trees about, treasuring the vast isolation and the privacy it granted them.

They had grown quiet, letting the breeze of the Canadian steppe fill the pavilion, the warm summer wind that would prevail briefly until this place turned fierce with cold and howling snow only a few short weeks from now.

"I wonder if I should go bald," he said suddenly.

"What!"

"Don't you think it would be better than this disappearing gray business I've got going on now?" He put his hand on the short crop of grizzled hair, the remainder in the losing the battle against the exposure of black scalp. He was sixty-seven, and his former abundance would never return.

"Wow, that's quite a bit of information." She smiled up at the white fabric. He was sure she was visualizing it.

"You wouldn't throw me out of bed if I were Mr. Baldy, would you?"

"Bed? When do we ever get to make love in a bed? Just in tents for quite some time now."

An exaggeration, quite charming.

"What do you call that fine room at the top of the Hyatt in Calgary five weeks ago? Seems like we almost broke that bed."

"That was someone else's bed. Doesn't count." She sniffed in disdain. "You know, our own bed, the marriage bed, the love chamber, the big four-poster of my dreams, like that."

"I would be bald."

"In your dream, you would be bald and I would be turned on. In my dream, I am in my very own bed, and you are turned on. Now exactly whose dream will you be starring in tonight, Mister?"

A tongue full of sass. He loved that. Part of the afterwards of lovemaking, her feisty-girl came out.

"I would take a lot of ribbing at the office. Bunch of jackals."

"It doesn't matter if you are the all-fired find-em-where-they-ain't star, and anyway the boss of the place?"

"Still no respect."

"You could threaten them, if they didn't stop mocking you, you'd keep the next big lake of black gold you found a secret."

"Not a big enough deterrent."

She went silent. He rose up to look in her face. Those deep brown eyes, clear and cool. Her smooth skin like wet velvet, blacker even than his, like some rare element of the earth, exquisite. She was a little stunned, glancing at him, now squirming with a look that had sex in it.

"What?" he said.

"Nothing."

"What?"

She licked her lips. There was no doubt about that expression – he had seen it so many times. He put his hand on her belly and she jumped. A breath she had been holding hissed out.

"I just got a picture of you bald ..." she began. More squirming. "... and you were, you know, between my legs."

He saw the light. No more rasping hair there. Just shiny bald pate. More skin to bring into contact with her most intimate skin. Oh my my my my my.

He went hard.

"A-ha, now we sing a different tune." He moved his body over hers, deliberately trailing the length of his cock along her thigh, making her take a sharp breath. Her hands came up behind his head and tried to pull him in. Instead, he dropped down her body and put his open mouth right below her belly-button and began kissing, slow, wet and sensual.

"If I were bald right now, I would kiss lower," he teased

Instead, the kiss moved like a procession back up her abdomen. His cock pressed against her lower leg, then higher, and when his mouth began to take first one and then the other soft breast inside, putting the nipples under his tongue, the cock urged itself against her thigh again, already thrusting in a damnable sexy motion.

Her arms got their wish. They circled his shoulders and pulled him tight. His mouth reached hers. He sensed her legs wide open under him. He insinuated his cock everywhere, against her belly, her legs, and slipped it time and again along the outside mound of her sex lips, quivering in supplication. She tilted perfectly to one side. He matched, the other way. Her mouth accepted his kisses as if a dripping flower to be searched for its nectar.

He edged the tip of his cock into the opening, melting slowly into her sex. The muscles gripped him, squeezed him and urged him on.

"Put it in deep," she implored.

There on the desolation much visited by ice, their animal screams echoed against the terminal moraine of the vanished ice sheet and fled over the empty earth, the mating cries of its wildest beast.

~~~~~

Monday morning, they watched him cross the tarmac from his parked aircraft. He strutted proudly. His head shone stark raving, in-your-face, nada, totally bare. He looked ten years younger. He swung open the door and the yells and caterwauls began. He made a circling motion with his hand, inviting them to come on, give your best shot. They did not fail in this. Finally, he held up his palms and they quieted.

"Enjoy yourselves if you must, people." He gave them a look of savage glee and raised a hand to his smooth, round black head.

"I am the happiest man alive on the face of this earth."

girl in love

She glanced into the bedroom.
Yes, still true.
Boy in bed.

She drifted back to the bathroom. In the mirror ...

Long fingers of one hand slipped across her cheek, as if to assure by touch this reality was real. Wide eyes disbelieving disbelief. Hair – run amok. Face – bare ... he insisted she wash everything off. A bite mark at the base of the neck flared purple-yellow, a trophy earned in retaliation for inflicting a love wound on his hip.

She stood staring at the reflection's stunned visage, its self-possession scattered with no urge to find the pieces to stitch itself together. She was merely that god-awful sappy-happy female person in the mirror, naked and limp.

Girl in love.

He arrived at the door of the bathroom. She

turned to show him the femme from the mirror.

"Fucking beautiful," he said.

"Yes."

His first step broke the spell. She offered open arms that drew him into embrace and pulled him against her body, including the inescapable male member. It sizzled, the shock of his skin on hers everywhere, his smell, his possessive hands on her back, murmurs of pleasure in his throat, and a fat, open kiss – so good she felt queasy in her belly.

The embrace broke up. She slipped into the shower, into its hot storm.

"Feels so good," she called over the shower door.

"Did you sleep well?" he asked.

"I have no idea. You mean this is not still sleeping?"

"This is no dream, this is really happening."

"Feels so good."

He stepped in behind, his body pressing with weight, insistent. So natural when embracing from behind for hands to circle and enfold breasts.

With a sigh, she leaned back against his chest, letting him touch as wished, hands slipping over soapy flesh with full mounds slithering in and out of his fingers. He kept aiming the nipples into the center of his palms, shifting back and forth, testing if they would make a dent. The cock throbbing against her bottom grew harder now – because of how completely she gave her body.

"Take everything ..." she murmured.

That made him spin her around and take her mouth. He moved in, all-the-way in, kissing surrendered places, skidding his tongue under hers. They twisted under the hot cascade of water.

Minutes later, they had washed all over, shampooing each other's hair. Hers was long and demanded a lot of regard. She became aware of how much he liked that. A surprise.

Now they were drying each other, knowing this was but an interlude. While teasing with all her might, his restraint did not budge.

Just slam me against the wall and nail me to it with that thing!

She finally overflowed, ran into the bedroom, threw off the towel, and launched herself with a screech onto the bed, landing face down, pounding her feet into it, churning against the sheets. She looked over her shoulder, saw him approaching, cock jutting stiff and strong.

She screamed with outrage. "It's going to fuck me."

He laughed. "Well, you're belly-down, legs locked, face in the pillow, so I'd say it's doubtful."

She turned her head to look up, suffused with laughter. "It's too big," she said, "you can't get that in me."

"Oh no?"

"I'm just this little thing. That must be for someone else. It's too big."

"Okay, I'll just put it away," he said, mocking broadly, turning away.

"No no no no no! Come back, come back, I didn't mean it," she pleaded, laughing.

He turned and marched right to the edge of the bed. She sobered. With eyes big and heart in throat, she spoke quietly.

"Put it in me."

"Turn over," he ordered.

She rolled onto her back.

"Open your legs."

Thighs parted, hips sank into the bed. She shifted to make room for him, creating the space where he would be. Slowly, achingly, her femme-heart thumping with safe-risk, a feeling so good she must go slow to make it wonderful, she exposed her sexual center.

Immediately he moved above, engaging her eyes. The big sweet shaft opened the lips, put its head inside, and in one smooth stroke, plunged to the bottom, pushing her wet insides apart.

Her stomach dropped with a thrill like a fall into space.

"Oh my God ..."

Her flesh flowed around his organ as if liquid – thick liquid sex. The vagina fit its muscles in place and squeezed down, once, twice, again – utterly carnal in intent.

He held still.

"Do that again."

She squeezed him tight.

"Can you do it a thousand times?"

She nodded, dreamy seduction in her eyes. She contracted again – and again – watching to see the effect, greedy to make his mind cream over.

She knew what to give, this time. "Don't wait for me," she whispered. "Put it in how it feels good and go all the way. Don't stop." She gripped around him, so tight, so good. "I'm going to keep squeezing."

He drew out. The tip stopped an inch above the parted lips, then poised between, hesitating. She didn't breathe. Then, the thrust, quick and deep, the passing making her insides ripple. She raised her hands to his neck and circled him gently, moved her fingers in his hair, and with a sigh, surrendered her body.

Later she would go for fireworks for herself, but now – to give him his way. She absorbed the rhythmic thrusts, looking down to see the exact juncture of his erection pushing through the lips, pouty and swollen.

"...being fucked silly ..." she murmured, as if observing a lucky girl other than her.

She kept up her contractions, content to stay close at hand, to be holding her legs apart, brilliantly aware of allowing a man to penetrate her opening, his erection jolting her entire sex, fucking her, fucking her so good, fucking her.

Her body shook to the root with each plunge of male strength.

Soon he reached the inevitable end, roaring into the air of the small bedroom, arching his back, and with the magnificent power of a wild beast – one she held serenely in her arms – slammed his cock a final time into her core.

The man-beast collapsed on her. She circled warm arms and legs around him and pulled, urging his full weight to crush down. His cock, if anything, went deeper than ever. Hard for a moment longer.

Her mind lit up with a sweet wanton question: what kind of a girl would keep her heart soft, tell him to take everything, spread her body wide, adore his penetrations, and beg to be fucked so much?

Girl in love.

see in

burn.

Revved up by three days of ocean plunges in high surf windward on Maui, voracious food runs, and numerous rides on top – still she could not exhaust lust. Even waking him in the night provided no relief. Now, a profound morning orgasm from stark physical sex ... that settled nothing. She had reached a height of vivid libido – a burn.

Emerging from the bathroom naked, slipping under the covers, looking him right in the eye, she reignited the drama.

"Let's do it again."

"Ayiiyi," he said. He squinted in disbelief.

She squinted back, to bring her unchaste urges into focus and inflict them on him.

"Again?" he asked.

"Guess that last one was pretty good," she admitted.

"Your legs were shaking."

"They were?"

"Quaking."

The burn roared up. Is the fire in her pelvis from the last, or the ignition of the next? She dropped a red coal of it on the bed.

"What if that was just a good scream on the way up? What if I don't want to cool off? What if I want to come again? And again?"

He took the edge of the sheet and in one motion stripped it off, spilling it onto the floor, leaving them naked except for a ring each on the best fingers.

The organ of concern jutted erect, waving with arrogance. The sight of the rampant rigid raging thing made her mind go white with greed ... slow, simmering greed.

"I'm in charge," she whispered.

He met her eyes, then nodded.

"I want to show you."

In slow motion she opened her legs, slipping one over his hip, pulling behind the knee of the other to part thighs out of the way.

"Right here," she said, lifting her bottom from the bed, rotating her pelvis in a small circle. "Here," she said, fingers on the lips. "Don't you like to see it after you just fucked it?"

"Mohh..."

"... after you just fucked it."

She caressed the lips and folds, deliberately causing the sound of wet parts sliding together.

"See in."

Her fingers parted the lips, slid deep, and pulled open to reveal the interior, the coral-colored rills shining with luster of syrup. Surely, he could see the opening of her womb nestled deep.

"Your cock, all the way in. It loved me sweet all night and then it pounded me raw when the sun came up – hard honeymoon sex in the morning."

"You're turning yourself on, the way you're talking."

"That's right," she answered. His eyes came up to find hers. With a tug of triumph, she saw he had fallen into a sexual spell. When a woman makes a man fall in, it turns her shameless – she will say things.

"Kiss it and drink it and fuck it ten thousand times. That's why we are married."

"Whoa."

"I love it, so sweet, so sweet, to keep the lips open, and one of them rubbing just right ..." she could not speak for a moment "... and oh, the ache."

"What?"

"Touching it makes it ache. It hurts so good, scary good. Like a burning ache somewhere in there. It aches so good. I'm afraid nothing can put out the fire. How did you get a woman to burn like this?"

She shut thighs tight. Her hand stayed in the vee, stroking. Its sensuous movements made her hiss.

"Show me again," he said. A tiny catch in his voice.

They shifted on the bed. Her leg slipped off

his hip and she opened to the fullest -- flat-out
spread wide as a woman can get. Her left hand
joined the other in between. Its fingers went in
the opening as well. She moved slowly. He
followed this dance with fascination. It made a
thrill in her heart to see him watching, to see
him adoring her sex. She delicately pulled the
lips apart again.

"Are you in love with it too?"

A pause ... stunned dumb by the flow of
flesh.

Then, "Yes, I love it," he said.

"In love with it all swimmy and spread open,
where you just fucked me?"

"Yes."

"Clit happy." She contracted her pelvis
around the ache.

"Yes."

"It's lying in its little nest, like a pink pearl,"
he said.

She moved the forefinger of each hand to fit
at the sides of the nest, used them to urge the
pearl up and away, a femme-way of getting
more erect. She did this for seconds, hissing and
cooing while he watched. Occasionally she
pulled the surrounding flesh away and down,
while two other fingers kept the opening
parted.

"That makes it really stand out," he
reported. "It's beautiful."

"So beautiful you fall in love."

He nodded.

"Every time you thrust in, it pulls on my clit. I love that. And sometimes when the angle is right, you rub it and bang it a certain way, it drives me right up the fucking wall."

"Let me in now."

"'By morning the groom was thoroughly shocked how rude the bride liked it'."

"Let me in now."

"She was still sweet though."

She slipped fingers out, folded the lips back against the mound with fingertips, exposing the pink, making a display.

"Put your cock right here," she said, "but not in."

He came above and pressed the shaft against the open lips.

"Now mister cock can fall in love with it," she said, engaging his eyes with her guileless ones. "Slide it up and down. I'll make it all wet." Her fingers held open the sensitive folds perfectly for the rubbing to provoke arousal. Wonderful how deep the ache reached, which told how strong the next orgasm would be – deep in her ass, her back, her pelvis. Even in her belly. All alive with sweet warm pleasure-pain, waiting to come.

"Put it in," she said, releasing her hands, bringing her arms up to circle his neck.

He moved the tip into place. Then the

penetration.

"Oh oh, oh yes."

It filled so full, pushed her insides around.
She squeezed tight and slid him deeper,
savoring the salacious flow of slippery wet
flesh. She whispered in his ear, "Right in my
fucking cunt."

"Yes."

She slid her legs nearly together, instructing
him to put his knees outside hers.

"Come up high," she said. He inched up on
the bed, forcing his cock deep, sliding his hips
up on hers. She adjusted beneath him.

"Don't pound me, this time. Use your
weight, let me feel your weight, but don't
pound, just rub me good."

He began a rhythm.

*He has to feel that ... hardness rubbing
against the lips, against the little nest, against
the button that feeds the ache. Squash me. Rub
me and squash me. Hurt it sweet.*

"Can you feel the lips?" she whispered.

He nodded.

"This way is for them, rub them, rub my clit.
Do me good."

He took it up instantly. She helped direct
through moans and urgings. His cock would
slip out halfway, then slide in strong. His
weight and this position high astride her hips
forced the penetration deep. He didn't pull out
at the end of each sinking, but rather rotated

his hips, making the base of the shaft and his hard mound inflame her sex.

The ache grew enormous. She felt it ignite her core. Fire flowed up her spine. They lasted long, enduring the excruciatingly slow ascent. They laughed together, seeing how high up they were. She must say her self-love again – no mercy from lust that burns. She held her eyes steady and true for him to melt with. He did not look away. Their love flowed there, aroused.

"I love my cunt," she whispered.

"Beautiful rude."

"... the willing bride."

"I feel like I'm in up to my waist," he said, grunting with each entry.

"Fuck it good. Love me. Fuck me ..." She went silent to let several thrusts penetrate to her cervix. Her torso arched off the bed to meet him. Three slow massive strokes ... she cried out ...

"OhFuck – OhFuck – OhFuck."

She recognized the point of no return, but it passed so slowly, not like the usual bursting followed by a crash. Instead – a calm, wide lake, warm and welcoming, exquisite. With each stroke of her lover she surged through the water, sailing away, with music of liquids streaming past her body, and a warm rain.

The ache spread through her pelvis, up into her chest, into her very breath. It ceased to torment, instead filling her heart with searing goodness.

Then it was in her throat. She screamed.

The water itself melted, and she with it.

All burning, all aching, drowned.

how quiet you can be

"I'm getting used to how quiet you can be," he said.

She smiled from the passenger side. A moment passed.

"See, you didn't even say 'yes' to that."

"No," she said.

This bit of flirty banter danced around the car.

Some men wish women would just shut up. It is axiomatic for them. Evidently, he had strayed into the wish-come-true zone of such men – do not tease her, she would be as quiet as a butterfly. And therein an irony – no woman so eager in bed could be thought shy.

This was a happy sexual femme who spoke almost nothing of herself, and even less about their new entanglement. He had not seen her texting, let alone phoning, during their first twenty-four hours. Her after-talk consisted of smiles. He did not even know if she had a cat.

As silent interludes continued piling up, his internal astonishment thickened – he was not the type of man who wished women would shut up.

He decided to call her bluff. They would arrive at Café St. Jacques in ten minutes. He made an unspoken vow to not be the next to speak.

Yesterday evening began as a test-the-chemistry meet, then moved from touch-dancing into first-time sex in the night, then showed no sign of being only-time sex – she remained in his bed. He made no attempt to force that one moment when the other sees she is invited gracefully to depart.

He found himself absent regret at dawn – on waking and hearing the shower, his unguarded center leapt with excitement. It took no time to fly in and yank the glass door open. She turned, threw arms around his neck, and engulfed him under the storm of hot water in a ravenous kiss, signaling demand by overt display of wanton female hunger.

He thumped her against the wall of the shower for that. For taking before he could take. For showing no shame. For wearing confidence of her confidence when naked.

For not talking.

One of his hands fit against her lower back just where the s-curve of a woman begins. He pulled her hips forward and rolled his organ over her belly. She arched in hissing escape. He put his other hand in her wet hair, twisted her head back down with intent, and opened her mouth with his, roaming it without inhibition, to leave nothing of it untaken. She squirmed. He used his hand to steady her head, to get perfect angles for dominating her mouth with his lips and tongue.

Two shining-wet bodies tangled by lust.

He pulled back. "I'm going to devour you."

She wriggled free and stepped out of the shower, with one piercing glance back. He washed quickly where it mattered, picked up a razor, rapidly worked his face with soap, and shaved off the night's growth, then dried off and strode into the bedroom.

The bed dominated, a blank square, a small stage with nothing but a clean naked woman prone upon it. In the three steps it took to approach, the legs of this creature flew open, creating the V-shaped nexus that beckons a man. He fell upon the bed, circled his arms around her hips, yanked her body a foot forward, and buried his mouth right at the center.

She screamed.

No other agenda in the act, no intent to ever stop, no heeding the groans and wild cries – only his mouth and tongue ravishing the splayed-open sex surrendered to him with entire consent.

He roamed the lips, sucking them, pushing them apart, rocking up and down with tongue inside, on each upstroke covering more and more

of the flesh at the high point, where the fine
shining pearl pushed out of its nest. This thing
wanted most attention – her hips swiveled to
make that point, in no mood for teasing. He got
his lips around it with unmistakable purpose and
pulled the sweet thing up, out, and around. It
fired off shuddering clutches from her pelvis into
her belly, reaching into her throat, which called
out, quavering. He would not relent, tugging
and slathering the inflamed button.

Abruptly, he pulled off, inched down to
spread the opening with his lips, and pushed his
tongue in, up against the roof, against the inside-
underside of the clitoris, and laved it once, twice,
again. She shrieked with wild abandon.

*You want to hear screams, you want to plant
your mouth right where desperate triggers lust for
it – you want to swim in melted sacred cunt.*

He stayed inside, assailing that one spot, until
he knew she could not return. When her voice
fell an octave, he dropped his mouth with no
mercy right on top of the glans. She went
gorgeously unhinged, bellowing something
incoherent, arching her back off the bed,
grabbing behind her thighs to pull her legs high
and wide.

He devoured her now, indeed, relentlessly, her
scent and taste inflaming his drive, holding right
through her highest screams, taking the liquids of
expending female release through all her descent,
pushing his tongue inside to feel the violent

contractions emanating from the bottom of her vagina. Every quiver – thrilling. He made no further move while she sailed free and the trembling continued.

She did something fine. Without a word, she pulled away, flowed over onto her belly, as one whose very flesh seemed itself thick liquid, and slowly, with aching gracefulness, raised her bottom. The knees spread apart. One hand appeared from beneath to fit the engorged vee, two fingers slipping inside, the others separating the lips so he could see. She looked over her shoulder at him, face suffused with naked beauty from orgasm.

"Fuck me," she whispered.

He moved into place and found an angle for his cock to slant up. She pulled the opening wide with two fingers. Then his only reality: sinking in, falling in. Her organs flowed around him. That moment of perfect connection, that elemental question 'where must I be,' all settled.

Now they were turning left off the avenue into the bistro's parking area. The carnal recollections of the day lingered on his mood.

"I'm hungry," she said.

He brought the car to a stop and turned as if to respond. She held his gaze easily. If she had been aware of his inner arousal over the past minutes while he recalled their trysting, she showed no sign. He let it become more obvious in his face.

"This is great sex," he said.

Her smile, a softening of the mouth, only. She must be simmering – in addition to their raw morning romp, they had joined again in late afternoon, slowly this time, with soft touch and enduring satiation. How ideal to walk out into the world, to seek fine food, after chasing each other up and down a bed until juices flowed.

Out and circling to her side, he drew her from within. Wisps of hair flowed over the collar of her coat as she lifted her eyes, arching up to offer her mouth. They made a small slow kiss, a warm amuse-bouche.

Inside, they were shown to a table remote from the bar, at his request being seated in back, a separate section away from one or two other tables occupied at this early hour, fitted into a corner behind a partial divider of the room. This afforded a little privacy.

The host who had seated them departed, having set menus and the wine list on the table. They did not open them.

"As asked, I've never been here before ..." he said.

Earlier, after naming 'seafood' as her preference, she had added 'Don't take me anywhere you've taken another woman.' Umbrage surged for a second before the cool fine sting of so confident an utterance overwhelmed it – a challenge clean as a whistle.

"... but I chose this restaurant on reputation for seafood. They have a specialty, Coquilles Saint-Jacques, we'll split a portion, then maybe sole sauté meunière? And definitely wine. Acceptable?"

"Oh, yes," she agreed.

"I want to go for it on the wine. To pull it all together."

She fell back against the banquette with an intrigued smile in place. He named the wine, and she gave an audible gasp. Her smile broadened, then a nod. He was sure it was full of irony.

He attracted the attention of the waiter, a request to send the owner for the wine consult. It was confirmed that indeed their products, and especially the sole, were impeccable, of quality to match his wine over-reach: Grand Cru Domaine Chablis Les Clos. This set off an amusing but contentious half-Gallic tussle over the vintage. He shut it down by declaring 'price no object, the best.'

They were about to scurry away when he stopped them on a signal from his companion. She leaned over and whispered in his ear. He controlled his surprise.

"Mademoiselle asks ... we request you bring nothing for at least ten minutes, in fact that we have the table with no visits for any reason. For ten."

They agreed with a nod and departed. 'The wine must chill anyway,' was certainly a part of their stoic acceptance.

With no seeming pressure, she hovered. His delight in her ways continued. Could their multiplication stay equal to her inventions in bed? He hoped.

Beat me at both games. Surprise me no end. I am caught by the mystery of you. And the sweet-wild sex. You are making me fall in love.

At the ripe moment, she spoke.

"Have you heard that some people are visual, some are auditory?"

"Yes."

"I am olfactory." She waved her hand in a circle before her face. "I know by scent."

"This dinner will be quite enjoyable, then."

"Yes. You have no idea. Also, I am gustatory."

Taste.

"What it means for me, always, is connection primitive, connection unseen by others, yet which pulls me into the maelstrom. I have had to learn when to decline despite a fire in the nose and honey on the tongue, and when to surrender."

"How do you do that?"

"The deployment of faculties far less romantic."

"Wait a minute. The way you put things. You were born in Europe. I'd bet it."

"Yes."

"Your English is fine, the accent is very endearing, but you are translating. And everything you say is florid. It's like you are a French poet from another century."

She smiled enormously and nodded in delight, eyes wet.

"I was born not thirty kilometers from where the wine you chose was born."

"No!"

She nodded. "Yet I refuse to say it was the only thing I drank as a child after completing sustenance from maman."

They burst out laughing together. It was so perfectly perfect. An incredible convergence.

Then she sobered.

"You must see how the anticipation of this repast, and the way you assembled it, and the *désaccord* over the vintage, have pierced me."

"Yes," he said. Apparently, it also loosed her tongue for talk. Stunning that twenty-four hours later the casual knowledge was just now catching up to the carnal.

"Last night, when we held close dancing, and when kissing began?"

"Yes?"

"All the fire and honey was there."

He moved his head close to hers. He grew aware of tiny movements that had been there all along – to increase the senses, aim them.

"You can taste me? Now?"

"I can taste our chemistry. And I know its scent."

Slowly he brought his mouth near hers and

held. She fit to him, brushed a kiss on his lips. They separated, leaving it delicately in place.

"Oh," she sighed.

What savor is that, what color the honey?

"Also, I have done something to enhance my knowing of you."

"What?"

"With sex, you must imagine what it does to me."

"Oh my God."

"Yes. This afternoon, after your last, you did not notice, I made my hands wet with it."

She looked deep in his eyes.

"It lingers still. I did not wash it away fully. I have you here."

She brought her hands to her face, turning them, inhaling.

"Oh ..."

"Tonight, when the after-sensations of this beautiful dinner have been enjoyed for hours, I will seek direct renewal of the other ..."

He could not speak, heart in throat.

"... on my hands, my breasts, and on my mouth."

the call of the great beasts

Today would be mildly ambitious – a few hundred yards to the trailhead, then winding a mile along West Maroon Creek to Crater Lake, where he would insist on stopping. Then, the serious stretch of the day, far into the U-shaped basin skirting Maroon Bells Peaks, the valley carved by a glacier that retreated ten thousand years ago. It would require most of the morning to hike to the head of the valley, followed by the climb up one shoulder. Tonight's camp was slated for West Maroon Pass, elevation 12,500 feet. To arrive, they faced less than six miles overall and a vertical gain of 2500 feet, a serious incline, but not a technical challenge.

She was taking to the mountains. Wisely, they had lingered two full days in Aspen for acclimation to the altitude. This had been preceded by four days in Denver, itself a five-thousand-foot jump-up from her accustomed La

Jolla, a town nestled on a cliff over the Pacific
Ocean in Southern California.

He watched her pulling gear from the vehicle
– tall, flexible, healthy, and absolutely sixty, a
wise sixty, with a shock of white hair framing a
face making no excuses for experience and
intelligence written in signs unmistakable.
However, the penumbra of her soul, her person,
was of youth, fresh and happy.

"Can I say it one more time?" he asked.

She laughed. The task of checking gear on the
tailgate of the Jeep stalled. She put her hands on
her hips in mock disapproval.

"Go ahead, come on, tell me one more time."

"This is the most beautiful valley in the world.
I can't believe you're finally going to see it."

"It's amazing you aren't worried about me
being underwhelmed. What if you strike out?"

"I won't," he said, soberly. He knew the vista
waiting for them, only a mile from here, could
not fail. It was his favorite place of all, for good
reason.

They finished checking everything, locked the
Jeep, and disappeared into the aspen trees.

At six-thirty that evening they reached West
Maroon Pass. Down the other side, west and a
little north, lay the back yard of the Maroon Bells
Wilderness, including the route of the fine hike
to Marble, Colorado, they would undertake
tomorrow. To the northeast lay the magnificent

valley that had delighted them all day.

She had been appropriately wowed by the two lakes and the view up the vale. The U-shape was so perfectly appreciable, and so uniform side to side, it almost seemed man-made. But on such a scale – it was stupefying. She sang a little joy-song at the sight of the Maroon Bells, two majestic peaks marching in a row like the king and queen, and a bishop with a tall hat lying down. And Crater Lake, clear, cold, serene, a mirror reflecting the occasional puff of cloud floating in the high blue sky.

Her halts for moments of silence and respectful contemplation confirmed his guess about the impact this hike would make. She had telegraphed her likely reaction months ago, when he visited last in California and watched her stand against the wind in rapt respect for nearly an hour as a storm sent the tide against a jumble of rock at the base of La Jolla Cove, for a violent and dramatically destructive afternoon. He had fallen in love with her that day, watching her watch the sea.

"Okay, okay ... that's enough ... of this straight up stuff," she said as they reached what obviously qualified as 'the top' in the near vicinity, although peaks towered above the pass in all directions. "I'm done."

She might be gasping for breath, but her face flushed with pleasure.

"Yes, but worth it, you've got to admit," he

said.

"I suppose ... you want me ... to ohh and ahh ... all ... all over the place now ... right?"

"Just wait 'til you look back."

She dropped her gear, including everything attached to her belt.

"Not yet."

He scouted the area, one in which camps had frequently been made. No firewood here above the tree line. That was expected. He would get them through the night without. He found a recess two-hundred feet off the trail, and lugged everything to it. She sat on a rock, absorbing how high up she was, he believed. He returned to her side.

"Let me show you something," he said.

"No more climbing."

"Just a little. It's worth it."

An insincere groan, although she had recovered nicely, he saw from her steady breathing. She looked him straight in the eye with those blue ones of hers, outrageously amplified in their intensity by the current environment.

"Thank you for bringing me up here."

She sidled nicely up to him, slipped arms around his neck, and lit a meaningful kiss.

Yes, and very well.

They hiked north along the pass-ridge, because he knew of a prospect rock jutting into the air above the valley of today's wonderful

walk. When she inched out on it to peek at the
valley floor a half-mile down, he had to laugh at
her reaction.

"Ooh."

Dark engulfed them a few hours later, such a
night as she had not seen in forty-five years, she
said, not since her teenage nights at camp in the
Sierra Nevada. No moon – it would not rise until
at least three in the morning, and no background
light from cities to haze the blackness, no sound
on this windless rock, not a cricket, not a drop of
running water, not a crackle of fire.

Above them wheeled the magnificent heavens,
the band of the Milky Way like a smear of vast
clouds, studded with brilliant solitaires
throughout. The familiar constellations glowed,
seemingly an easy reach away. She put her hand
to the sky to try once or twice. The blackness
held out infinite millions of stars, millions as he
had never thought could be seen by human eyes,
even from a mountain. Low across the valley,
between two peaks of the White Mountains, the
most dazzling thing in the sky kept drawing their
attention – Jupiter, rising in the east.

She asked for them to be naked, under the
naked sky, wanted starlight glinting in her wild
white hair, to see it in his eyes.

She accepted him inside her body early. They
did not care about satiation, but rather the
joining, and would stop moving now and again,

holding still, sitting facing, joined indeed, listening, listening to the silence. They could see into each other's eyes because of so many stars shining on them. This was thrilling.

She put him on his back on a mat they had brought, arched over him and moved her sex slowly up and down on his. It was so gentle, so arousing, he could hardly keep from lunging back. She made him take it for long minutes, painting him on the outside before guiding it in. He made her lift off completely several times for them to savor the glimmer of stars in the wetness on his organ, her wetness on him.

It was not long after dark when it was too cold to lie out in the open. He had a tiny heater going inside their tent. It was just enough for them not to have to put on even a shirt.

"I want to stay naked all night," she said, maneuvering inside.

"It will be much colder soon. This warm, this high, even in August, is unusual."

"We have down bags for that, though."

"Um ... heat is not going to be a problem in this tent tonight."

She smiled at his irony, then sobered. "Be inside me again."

He moved slowly. He rubbed himself all over the ripe flesh between her legs. She rubbed back. They slid their parts together like teens kissing. He took his cock in hand and eased the head just inside the lips, opening her, making room, getting her to hiss and beg. He rubbed it high against the place where the lips joined, and her favorite spot waited. "My happy button," she called it. She got him to use the tip of his organ to push against it, many times.

"Please," she whispered, finally.

Holding her gaze, he eased himself all the way in, right in. Her legs circled his hips like an angel enfolding. Slowly and sweetly, they lifted off into an otherworldly realm, sacred and luscious, so right, so strong. Her body accepted each stroke with a squeeze and a tilt of the pelvis. This time they allowed the deliberate mounting of arousal, the sure climb up.

She shifted further under and moved her legs higher, a way of asking for his cock to touch a certain place at a certain angle. He rocked it home, there, again and again.

Both began to cry out, moans that contained words, the beautiful carnal poetry of sex. The sounds of their pleasure echoed across the path and perhaps filled the ancient glacial hollow below them, like the call of the great beasts that roamed the valley before the ice came.

They had pulled the down sleeping bags around them. He was sure she would sleep through until morning. But to his joy, she woke him in the night for more sex. He was potent at once. His wish, when he felt his erection bloom, was to grow hard instantly – on her desire – for decades to come. That would keep them young.

They were so lusty they wanted the taste of each other's parts in their mouths, and found a position in the small space to enable it. Then, he turned her over, pinned her down with his legs, and plunged in deep. Within a few dozen strokes his final thoughts on the matter were said, with emphasis.

"Beast," she said

"You too."

She nodded in agreement. "It's good like animals, sometimes. Especially when I'm in heat and you are rutting."

He liked her talking this way. The frankness in it reinforced how real she was – this was. He decided her libido was immortal.

If only you knew how grateful I am to get you, at our age. You have not said it yet, but you have fallen in love.

A serene, serious expression settled onto her face. More than ever he saw in it simultaneously the sixty-year-old and the young soul. He felt infinite, gazing at it.

She unzipped the tent and stood up, taking his hand, pulling him behind. It was cold. A bright light filled the hollows of the rocks from a giant moon rising over the shoulder of the ridge across the valley, filling the landscape with dreamlike illumination, soft and creamy. Her arms lifted high, her back arched, and with a gesture of a pagan, she offered her body to the heavens, white with stars and the burning soft silver of the moon. She froze like this for seconds, her breath a cloud surrounding her face.

Then she lowered her arms and turned to him. The white lit up her body. He watched, fascinated, as she separated her legs a little, brought her hand between, and let several fingers fit along the labial ridge. He could see everything. She slipped part of her hand inside, easing the lips apart. With a deliberate contraction of the muscles of her groin, a small ribbon of liquids flowed down one thigh, directed that way by her stance and fingers. She raised the shining hand and moved it over her breasts, leaving a trail there. She put it to her face and inhaled.

"It's yours and it's mine," she said, holding the anointed hand out to him, face alight like a goddess overcome by the moon and filled with as fine a madness there could be.

love in bed

"I'm going to get sand in my hair," she said. They took in the primal scene for a beat of time. Then he grasped her hand and led them onward.

"I'll wash it again when we get back," he said.

They made their way down a low cliff-face, through a rocky strip, onto the shallow sand beach. The ocean greeted them, crashing and hissing with spray blown off waves expiring in this cove, a miniature basin with but eighty feet of frontage, at either end of which arose headlands extending out to sea.

A white sundress blew around her legs. The wind tugged at her straw beach hat trimmed with a lavender sash. He was already down to his bathing suit. The onshore flow of North Atlantic Ocean air tempered the otherwise high-eighty-degree heat. Just the way he liked it.

They anchored a blanket with a cooler-bag

and a canvas tote, and dropped a drawstring
satchel on a bottom corner. They applied lotions.
Lying down, he stretched out to let the sun begin
its baking, gratified with how less windy it was
near the ground. She preferred sitting with knees
bent, looking out at the ocean from beneath the
brim of her hat.

That was inevitable at the edge of the sea, to
gaze out, grasp the vastness, to apprehend the
strange otherness of being alive right at the cusp,
sounds and smells exotic. Most affecting – the
rhythmic pounding of the surf, good-sized
combers breaking on the edge of the continent.

For a half-hour, they did nothing but meld
with the beach. As expected, not a soul disturbed
them. That timeless feeling made its appearance,
teasing an invitation to a trance in which he did
not sleep, but sank into a thickness formed of
powerful ocean elements in their dominance. He
floated, unafraid, yet blinded by the glare of the
potent sun. Then a sea-surge lifted him high on a
crest, the roaring wave sweeping him with fated
certainty to the coastline. He regained sight – of
a sandy cove with mountains soaring beyond.
And her, seeking him along the lonely shore.

Shaking off this beach-dream, he flipped over,
then back again. Twice. An ironic grin
accompanied his agitation. He might be falling
deeper in love by the second, but his male body
did not consider it relevant – demanding sex
immediately, as flat as that, as if the fertility god

had simply marched out of the sea and tapped him on the shoulder to command: *sex*.

However, such a thing would not be easy. Normally they could light off a spark with indecent banter while touching under the sheets and she would melt in, ready willingness a thrilling aspect of her appeal. Here, little hope – his petulant will believed – she would accept his hand inside the sundress at best.

"Nobody's here," he said.

"Just us."

"I told you it would be really isolated. It's possible no one's been on this beach at all," he said. "Ever."

"Why not?"

"I don't think it's an official beach. No name. No organized access. Usually there's no sand here, just rocks and these headlands, but during April there were three big storms in fifteen days. I think they scooped up the sand and dumped it above the normal waterline like this. Instant beach."

"It's primitive."

"The only reason I know about it is because Jai clued me in. He was sailing down this shoreline, comparing his charts with GPS readings, and he saw this little cove and patch of sand. There was nothing on the map for it. But he had it located to the foot because of the GPS, so I figured out that detour from the road about a mile back. Worth it, I think."

To get to the cliff behind them, and thus to this beach, they had abandoned the narrow unpaved track paralleling the shore and crossed a grassy flat area in the Jeep, now parked out of sight.

"I feel like a castaway," she said wistfully.

They were quiet for a while, absorbing the fusion of salt air and hot sun on skin glistening with sunscreen and balming oils. His libido went into rough idle.

Then she removed her hat and sunglasses and lay belly down close beside him, smiling. With his emotions for her on the run-up, her light-hearted mood, and the nearness of her warming body – more than one chakra sighed.

She said, "Just now I had a second there where it really felt like we were all alone in the world. The last two. I can't feel anything happening anywhere else, there's only this spot. And us."

"No one to bother us," he said.

"No."

"I'm surprised you like that feeling, being that alone."

"With you, only. Don't you know a lot of women have that stranded-on-an-island fantasy?"

"You're kidding me."

"Nope. You don't know how much time we spend worrying about some other female wrecking everything, because we know men have the wayward eye."

"The what?"

"Wayward eye. Lots of women will exploit it just to do damage. You men will get hot for anything if you think you have a chance, so any girl on the make will strut around telegraphing her alleyways are open for business, and pretty soon she has a trail of dogs in heat, married or not, yelping behind."

"That's terrible." He pretended to sound offended by this cynical appraisal of love. He knew she did not actually believe it.

"But on the island, or wherever, there's no chance. I'm telling you, the idea that you can have your man with no troubles, no competition, that's really a hot fantasy for a girl, especially a young girl before she gets any power for herself."

"You have power."

"I know, but it's still hot to feel that twinge, you know, the two of you are alone, all alone, and you have him all to yourself. To do whatever."

She was grinning now, having confessed the guilty pleasure of indulging in such a clichéd scenario, not regretting the threat to her substantial credentials as an independent femme, apparently.

"Does this fantasy turn you on?" Might as well try.

Her eyes sparkled. She sat up. Wisps of hair blew across her face. She looked up and down the beach and out to sea. Then she stood and pointed to the cliff at the back of the cove.

"What about someone coming the way we did?"

"Doubtful. It's completely off-road and there's not supposed to be any beach here, remember? And no one can see the Jeep."

With that, she took on a new mood. She strolled down to the water, footprints made and washed away while skipping at the surf line. The dress flowed in the wind – she pushed her hair around with a hand once or twice. Then a big breeze blew up. Arching her back to breast it, throwing her hands to the sky, dress and long hair streaming behind, gloriously free in the sun, her voice gave out a high note of challenge into the teeth of the wind.

He resisted the urge to run to her. Shortly, she resumed her beach-dance, letting it carry her halfway back to the blanket, stopping ten feet away. The open rush of sun and wind had freshened her face and skin – she looked a creature of the wild shore.

A hand went to her shoulder and released the sundress straps, causing the top of the garment to fall to the waist, where one hand pinned it. The other pulled apart a bow on her bikini top, and with a little maneuver, it fell to the ground. Exposed to him and the entire absent world, her bare torso – slender, supple, with sweet breasts in proportion.

"Unfuckin'believable," he said, low under his breath. He still did not move, but now more 'frozen in place' than by any calculation. Luckily, she ignored his reaction, dancing around on the beach facing this way and that in turn, surely trying on the idea of being nude under the sky.

She stopped again, looking down at herself. She glanced at him. With a smile of finality, she eased the sundress off her hips, letting it slip to the sand. Determined, she pulled at the bow on the final garment and with one dramatic movement became completely naked. She tossed the dress across the space between them, where it settled on the blanket.

Instantly he was standing, yanking off his suit, striding to her. She backed away, laughing as if unafraid of any randy stallion. He did not have to chase her far. At the edge of the surf, they twined and kissed and pressed, tangling in each other's hair.

She spun around and arched her back to deliberately exaggerate exposure ... inviting him to cover with hands from behind ... to cup ... to sizzle with tight goodness in possession ... to savor softness and supple tenderness ... to tease the nub right at the top curve ... to once again celebrate that no one not under their spell could appreciate the fantastic eroticism of small breasts like he did.

Not even her.

"It's a nude beach now," he said.

"Only our nude beach," she whispered. "In paradise."

She spun around. His organ pressed her belly. She tilted her head and sought his mouth, whimpering when he pulled them tightly together. The kiss surged, enormous.

Suddenly, she jumped out of his arms and took three steps back. With outstretched arms, like Venus invoking the moment of first loving, her eyes searched the sky, then the dunes with beach grass waving, then over the horizon out to sea. She returned to stand directly in front of him. Her hands moved behind her back. She arched slightly from the waist to offer her body – so vulnerable in her nakedness it made him ache.

"Touch me," she whispered.

She locked eyes with him while his hand caressed her torso, her neck, her face. Her arms stayed behind her back.

"Touch me. Touch my body."

His hand moved down to her belly, then found the curve below. She swayed hips to fit his caress.

"There," she whispered, "Touch me. There. Touch there."

He took possession of the yoni as freely given. The meeting of their eyes, so fiery as he caressed intimately, moved arousal swiftly to the moment where it demanded sex.

Quick, give me a sign.

She pulled away again. She folded her arms

across her body. She spoke their beautiful consent word, agreed during their first day making love in bed.

"Everything."

He picked her up and carried her to the blanket. As he set her down, she rolled on top, grabbed the back of his head and slipped her mouth inside his, lips under his, tongue wild. This lit off an exquisite fire in his mind – she was aggressive in kissing rarely. It transported him to lust heaven when she kissed deep in his mouth. He slipped one hand around the back of her neck to feel her motions, and without an ounce of control, let the amazing, invading, female-forward kiss go on and on and on.

With one thigh over his lower body pinning his organ beneath, he was sure she would raise up and connect their bodies. What happened next was the sunniest of all hopes for this beach party.

"Wait...," she said.

She sat up, slipped hands down her legs, took an ankle in each, and pulled knees up to her chest. Falling back to the blanket, elbows fit behind knees and forced her legs aside and along her body. Hands floated between thighs. Fingers went to the rim of her sex, slipped in, and she eased the lips apart. A heart-breaking ballet.

"You can have me anytime you want, here on our deserted isle," she said. "I'm given to you."

A close thing – he nearly shot off from the thrill, could not look in her eyes. He knelt in place, leaned over, and slid his cock inches in. She fit fingers where the lips folded around the shaft, one fingertip slightly inside the orifice – to be touching there during penetrations, he realized with a shudder.

He fit his hands in the crook of each knee and allowed his weight to push.

"Can you take that?" he asked. She was limber, yet this was extreme.

"Go slow."

He engaged her eyes for guidance while their bodies shifted weight and accommodated bending as he pushed. Her knees and the tops of thighs went flat on the blanket. His cock worked deep, fully buried in luscious wet flesh.

Now her hands could really contribute, since the arms had no part in holding the position – she was pinned in place. The tendons in the back of her legs pulled aside the fleshly part of her thighs and bottom, so the mons, the clitoris, and the tender lips lay prominent, offered – utterly exposed.

He drew his cock out. Her fingers took the shaft and brushed its head around the outer lips. She caressed her clit with it. There was so much wet that every motion made a slushy sound, clearly audible despite the ceaseless sound of the sea. She used a sideways swirl with the tip inside to open herself more.

Then, he began a sweet, smooth stroke, in rhythm. The position was so pleasurable –

perfect for shallow quick ones, and others deep
to the bottom. The angle caused the head of his
cock to rub a spot inside on the roof of her
vagina. A good spot.

"There. Yes. There. Right. There." She
grunted, one word on each thrust. "There.
There. There."

It took only twenty or thirty strokes right *there*
to send her voice squealing, wailing off into the
sky. "Don't stop," she begged, voice pathetic
with desperation. "Don't stop don't stop don't
stop don't stop," then "please oh please oh
please." This mantra never let up while he
slammed into her, twenty, thirty, fifty more
times.

A final scream, bellowing desperation wild
with insanity. Her sex seized and shuddered. A
flood came down all through the organs. She
sailed high free and far in release, whimpering
out little round "oh" sounds in time with ripples
of pleasure surging through muscles.

She cooed deliciously in the aftermath for
many seconds. Her hands were full of juice. She
spread it on the half-buried phallus and all
around her clit, wiggling hips to set the
satisfaction deep in swollen flesh. He put his
endgame on hold.

Just as he thought she would unfold herself
from the extreme position, her shining hands
came up from below. She put them against her
face, inhaling. Then she turned them to him,

touched his face tenderly, leaving the scent
strong near his mouth. Her arms circled his neck
and pulled down.

"Crush me," she implored.

Beyond belief of what nature would allow, she
drew his torso down, even bent in half as she was.
He held his breath to savor contact with the
precious breasts. He released the tension in his
arms and thighs until she bore much of his
weight.

"Crush me," she said again, rocking to urge
him deeper onto her frame. He released his
weight fully. She moaned and thrashed,
squirming to find room to breathe. One hipbone
got leverage, just enough to lift him slightly.

"I want another one," she said, eyes sparkling
in the sun. Then her mouth came to his ear. She
whispered in it.

"I am your only in the world. Love me until
my heart hurts. Then fuck me a thousand times,
here at the edge of the sea."

His core erupted. He raised, pulled back, and
thudded forward. She screamed -- it lit off a
terrible urgency. He attacked with utter freedom
the undefended femme below. The wet grew
extreme now, an overflowing lake of hot juice.
Her enfolding organs constricted on each
plunge, the insides taut, but slick.

"... right there right there oh please oh please
oh please right there oh please."

He did not fail her pitiful prayer. His aim was

true, he was young and strong, his cock with glorious weight behind it stroked *right there*. Quickly a new cataclysm emerged in her ragged breath, her pelvis, and low in her voice of coming. Under his relentless plunges, she vaulted over.

His forborne ardor had let the thick flood flow, had taken her scent, let her thrash and scream. Now it would speak. He pinned her down as never before, reared back and thrust his organ deep, many times, to the mouth of the womb, where birthing muscles quivered in orgasm.

The sea lifted one last wave, a wall of water above which he could not see. He swam up its slope and knifed inside short of the crest. Wishing to drown – and not – his soul drank the liquor that runs salt-red in our bodies and makes us love.

He exploded through the far side of the wave. The infinite opened behind his eyes. Bellowing with madness, he let loose in that place his power, as the pounding sea had done, forever on the shore.

End
Love In Bed

Origin of three books
eyes full of light and laughter
touch me again
love in bed

Over twenty years beginning at the start of the 21st century, sixty tales of love escaped my romantic optimism and immoderate sexual imagination onto the page, now published in three volumes.

They might depict turn-of-the-heart moments – a first glance, a surrender, a smile of invitation, a mutual recollection – or the high drama of lovers risking emotional intimacy during sex.

That feeling and that feeling – with neither shy.

Absent: cheating, cold beds, cruelty, drift, unfair deaths, sophisticated boredom, and cynical scorn of love. Yes, such things exist in life, and much has been written of them.

Elsewhere.

Eyes Full of Light and Laughter, published under my pen name John Caedan, is considerably less explicit, sexually, then *Touch Me Again* or *Love in Bed.* Yet all sixty-two episodes are of one voice, of the same bright intention, and – I hope you will discover – of the same nakedness.

John Kirnan
Sonoran Desert, California, spring 2024

About this edition

Images:
model, composition, and render
by John Kirnan

Text font: EB Garamond
Designed by Georg Duffner, Octavio Pardo
for Google Fonts

Story titles font
Designed by Chad Savage

Text block style:
Ragged right, non-hyphenated.
While writers are strictly advised to format
their texts with equal length lines,
I inquired if that included poetry.
No.

by j.j.kirnan

jane nineteen
touch me again
love in bed
andrés + mila

jjkirnan.com
loveinbed.com

For more, please visit
LoveInBed.com

For most, please visit
patreon.com/loveinbed

Patrons receive ebook editions
of books, and exclusive access to
my most audacious
erotic writing.

by john caedan

eyes full of light and laughter
the preludes
the white sky
saraIRL

johncaedan.com